ThE StoNEFLoWER REVoLUTioN

I0769245

This is a work of fiction. Names, characters, places, and incidents either are the product of the author's imagination or are used fictitiously. Any resemblance to actual persons, living or dead, events, or locales is entirely coincidental.

Copyright © 2025 by Danielle Dexter

All rights reserved. Published in the United States by Cupid's Arrow Press. No part of this book may be reproduced or used in any manner without the written permission of the copyright owner, except for the use of quotations in a book review.

First Edition 2025

Cover design by C.A.P Designs

Paperback ISBN: 979-8-9918831-1-5
Alternative Paperback ISBN: 979-8-9918831-2-2

the stoneflower revolution

a 90s Nostalgia Novel

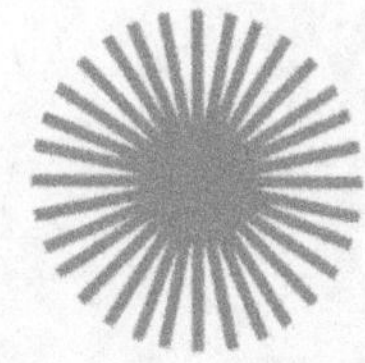

Danielle Dexter

Cupid's Arrow

PRESS

DEDICATION

To Nick, who always gave the best advice.
And to Tania who would have read this first.
xoxo

Cupids Arrow
PRESS

Backstage Pass with Luke Grant
Present Day

Chapter One
Now

My hand brushes against the strap on my luggage as the zipper slides along the seam, much like a train chugging on its tracks. There are only two directions to go, just like the train, but the obvious one is to keep moving forward. Nothing ever good comes from going backward. At least, that's what I've been told.

Some might say I was, in fact, going backward. But I didn't see it that way. My future was simply left behind like an object thrown into a lost and found box that only I could reclaim. Again, some might argue that some things are better left lost. But I didn't see it that way either. I believe only the passage of time can truly make that call.

Do you know that feeling when you've lost something like your favorite T-shirt or CD? And while you spend all your time searching for it, or finally accept that it's gone, you come across something you weren't even looking for? Well, that's my life. It's a collection of lost things I've spent countless years trying to keep from losing again. What hurts the most, however, is not knowing how lost I am to her. I wonder if she searches for me the same way I have searched for her. I hope that when the day comes when we find each other again, we find we never lost the feeling of what we once meant to each other. (To be honest, that's one thing I've managed not to lose.)

Everything else, like the memories of my life, has come to me like waves crashing against the edge of my mind. They pull back and recede as if they have carried too much to the shore. The ocean holds a lot, most of which has yet to be explored. I often think that the deeper you dive, the more you may uncover what you might not want to find. Maybe that's why I've stayed so long at the shallow end of my life.

I slip into a pair of jeans, thread my belt through the loops, then grab a T-shirt from my closet and pull it over my head. It's one of my early band shirts that my mom made for everyone before we hit it big. Some might consider the shirt "vintage" now, since the logo has faded from many washes. Yet, I still believe the 1990s were only a decade ago—and let me tell you, what a decade it was.

Nostalgia is a dangerous mistress—a relationship I have maintained for as long as I can remember. My memories often shift into what my heart can handle recalling, acting as a kind of defense mechanism. Sometimes, I am entirely to blame for this. Other times, I have no control at all. It's a wild dance where only I know the steps.

I style my messy hair with a little pomade and brush my teeth just before catching a glimpse of my reflection in the bathroom mirror. I look into the eyes of someone I barely recognize anymore. He appears very different from the person I used to be. For a middle-aged man, I can't help but feel like my internal clock is out of sync with my outward appearance. On the outside, I feel like I've aged gracefully, like a fine bourbon, but on the inside, I'm still fermenting. It's amazing how much time can change things, and even more incredible what it doesn't.

The press often says that I'm "young at heart." I'm not sure where they got that idea, especially since they once called me an "old soul." Maybe my personality has changed in a way similar to Benjamin Button? Still, it's safe to say that time hasn't really changed who I am at my core. It's like a strange dance where I alternate between being rooted and growing: a teenager with nothing to lose and an adult willing to lose it all.

There are moments when I hesitate, wondering if the version of myself now is one she could love, just as the version she once loved before. I've heard that you can love someone deeply—a preserved kind of love—that doesn't carry over into the present. It's a love you look back on but never move toward. I fear that the love she has for me now is this preserved kind—frozen in the past—where I am only loved through the memories she reflects on.

But here is where it all gets messy.

For so long, I've wandered through a sepia-toned world as if I am part of a distant version of myself that hasn't fully come into color. I should be grateful for everything I've achieved, but what good are those things if you have no one to share them with? Sure, I have my parents and friends, but it's not the same. And it hasn't been the same in a very long time.

However, I'm hoping to change all of that.

Slowly, my body sinks into my bed. My head touches the soft cotton fluff of my duvet, and for a moment, I feel like a teenager again. I'm full of promise, hope, and resilience. I can bounce back just as quickly as I fall. I'm full of untapped potential, angst, and emotions that seep into every fiber of my being before pouring out onto paper or through the strings of my guitar. I am full of unrestrained energy and passion. I'm returning to caring less about what others think of me and more about what I think of myself.

Man, I really miss those days.

Even better, I miss him.

Then again, do I really? Or am I just seeing things through rose-colored glasses again?

I often wonder if my memory is playing tricks on me, as if it's withholding important information that could change my perspective entirely. It's possible. However, I've been told that with proper help, those blank spaces in my life will never stay empty again. Like exposure therapy, I need to keep gradually reconnecting with my daily life. Unfortunately, like a dark room, I've kept the lights off for a long time because I've been too scared to face anything that might be overwhelming. So, I did what was best for myself: avoidance (so much for exposure). *With the lights out, it feels less dangerous.*

I hear you, Kurt.

It would be so easy for me to crawl back into bed and forget all of this since it's a mystery social media could easily solve. But I'm not one for that kind of connection. I felt way too exposed during the AIM years, so I'm not about to share every personal detail of my life for the world to see (which is an odd thing for someone who has spent the majority of their adulthood in the spotlight to say).

Whether it's the limelight, spotlights, or highlights, it's all just a show. For many years, I played the part of someone I knew wasn't my whole, authentic self. I wish I had given myself the grace to just *be*. There are many people we look back on in our lives, wishing we'd had the chance to hold onto them longer, but we rarely think about all the versions of ourselves we'd wish we could have done the same for. I wish I had held onto him longer. I wish I could have told him to be brave and that life is too damn short not to follow your heart.

There was a time in my life when I was complacent in many ways. I chose to settle instead of fighting because I hated confrontation. I feared rejection. I was also more worried about how others would feel, so I suppressed my feelings. I often wondered what certain parts of my life would have been like had I been honest with everyone. Would things have turned out differently? Or would they have ultimately led me to the same place, no matter what? It's a question I know I will never have an answer to, but it hasn't stopped me from wondering.

I didn't realize it at the time, but I had it made. Sadly, we don't always see what's right in front of us until we're waving goodbye to it in the rearview mirror. I'm not the first (nor the last) to think that time is endless. It's the curse of youth, I suppose, when you look ahead and see so much of it. So, you seize the moment. It's only as the years fly by, slipping through your fingers like sand, that you wish you could buy it all back and store it in tiny jars for later use. That's why I'm being cautious now, especially when it comes to how much I invest in others. I definitely can't ask the universe for a redo (because, man, do I have a laundry list there), because once time is spent, it's gone. Time, I've learned, is our most valuable currency, so spend it wisely on those who truly matter.

I roll over and close my eyes in deep concentration. I need to gather the courage to pull myself up. I can't give in to fear just because it's easy to surrender—like settling into a comfort zone. But there is nothing comfortable about the situation I'm in.

Sadly, I've been in this same spot before. I've packed this very bag. Like a vivid dream, my departure feels rehearsed in many ways. Yes, I control what I'm doing, but it doesn't seem real. Even when I make myself sit up in bed, it all feels like a recurring dream. Still, I have to wake up and face the music (in more ways than one).

Music is my life. It is the foundation of how I define myself. It goes hand in hand as if my guitar were an extension of me. However, lately, I have almost cut off that part of myself, creating a phantom limb that follows me around like a ghost, reminding me of the mess I left when I went away.

Catch that, Alanis?

Besides my guitar, lyrics tell my story. Everything you need to know about me is pretty much written in song form. Who needs a therapist when you have music? Well, truth be told, sometimes you need both.

Anyway, it all started back in 1997…

It was almost serendipitous, if you had asked me. The idea surfaced at a time when mainstream rock n' roll was paving the way toward grunge, alternative rock, and the emergence of what the early 2000s called "emo." The music made the listening crowd cheer, showing that selling out didn't mean selling out. It was a pathway to success, not the end of it, something we naturally feared, thanks to Kurt Cobain. I couldn't help but wonder what the impact on the music world would have been if he were still here. He was a rare talent taken too soon, and I'm just thankful for the time he gave us. Speaking of which, did you know that nirvana is a state of freedom from suffering? Ironic, isn't it?

I'll defer again to Alanis.

My feet embrace the carpet threads as they finally hit the floor in unison. I decide to take a final tour of my bedroom, looking through dresser drawers, closets, and peeking under the bed to make sure I haven't forgotten anything. I drag my bag behind me as it glides across the wooden floorboards, reaching the small hallway rug where it catches on a few loose threads. I brace myself for the noise as I continue dragging it down the stairwell. It bangs against each step, sounding like a drum solo that I'm only privy enough to hear.

Encore!

The sound echoes throughout the stairwell where I've hung various pictures over the years. I glance at a few before noticing the blank spot that holds space for a single nail. I remember the day I took down the picture that once called it home. I tossed it down the stairs and watched it shatter into a million pieces before one of my friends caught it to save the photo. All I wanted was for the picture to feel what I felt inside: broken. Clearly, no one understood the symbolism I was trying to convey.

Sometimes, I reflect on the deeper meaning of glass and how delicate it truly is. The broken shards that cut through my skin as I cleaned up my mess that day hurt less compared to the transparency of it all. The glass that framed the picture I had shattered revealed something to me that I couldn't physically touch. The pain from that hurt more because it left scars that no one could see. Sometimes, I think that's much worse because how can you heal something you can't see?

For years, I considered putting the picture of her and me back up, but over time, I realized I would rather walk across broken shards of glass than be reminded of what I couldn't touch.

Chapter Two
Now

The morning sky welcomes me like a warm hug from someone who has been there through all the ups and downs of my life. It's strangely comforting. Even though I've tried this trip about a hundred times before, I soon realize I have no plan. Still, it doesn't stop me from locking the door behind me.

I climb into my blue Ford pickup, a family heirloom of sorts that my father gave me after he left our family to start a new one. It seemed like he thought this parting gift would make up for his absence in my life, but instead of helping to bridge the gap, I used it to push myself further away. He never asked for it back, though. He was a man allergic to confrontation. I guess, in some ways, the apple doesn't fall far from the tree.

I turn the key in the ignition as the engine roars to life. My legs start bouncing up and down as if trying to shake off nervous energy. I rest my hands firmly on my knees, stopping all movement. Immediately, the sudden stillness causes my nervous system to behave like a makeshift pinball machine. The imaginary ball shoots through my entire body, not caring whether I want to play or not. When I finally look up, the inside of my truck is veiled in fog as though I am trying to see through a cloud of smoke. I grip the steering wheel tightly, then close my eyes and count to ten. I never thought it would be this hard.

For a moment, it feels like I can see her. She sits beside me in the truck, her long auburn hair flowing in the wind as we drive down back roads with music blaring. She turns to me and smiles, and all I can think about is how perfectly we fit together. We are two pieces of a puzzle—the lyrics to my songs. She is the muse behind everything I create, yet she has no idea how much power she holds over me. Then, as quickly as a flash of light, we find ourselves back in my teenage bedroom. The dark brown woods, the posters, and the soft glow of my lava lamp.

"Are you OK?" she asks as I pack up my luggage. Three months of touring felt much shorter before she came into the picture. Now, it feels like I will be gone forever. I doubt she feels the same, but a guy can dream.

I set my bag down and go to her. I wrap my arms around her tightly, as if I'm afraid to let her go.

"I'm proud of you. Do you know that?" She looks up at me.

"It means more to me than you would ever know." I nuzzled my face into her shoulder. I breathe in her Sun-Ripened Raspberry perfume by Bath and Body Works (a popular scent, but it only makes me think of her).

"I don't want to go," I say, fighting back tears that threaten to pour out like floodgates opening. She can't know how I really feel. I have to hold it together because last time, it nearly destroyed everything.

"You have to," she says to me. "You would regret it if you never took this chance. You all would."

"What about you?" I ask, listening to the muffled sounds of my bandmates from downstairs. I do my best to ignore their excited cheers and laughter as they hype themselves up for what they believe will be a life-changing, epic journey. Who would have thought that our small high school band would get this far?

"I'll be fine." She looks at me with eyes begging for reassurance. But she will be fine. It's me I'm not so sure about.

"Oh, and keep Dax in line, OK? I know how he loves to get into shenanigans," she laughs.

Once the muffled voices have mostly faded, I pull away from her and grab my bags.

"Do you have everything?" she asks.

I tilt my head at her. "Not everything."

She smiles because she knows deep down that this goodbye means more than either of us dares to admit. There is so much left unsaid in the words unspoken. It's a melody that touches the heart more deeply than those three little words ever could.

But those three little words linger in the air with a clear question mark. If either of us dared to mention them, it would become a promise, one that could be given with or without reciprocation.

Somewhere between us falling in and out of love, the question has escaped my lips more times than I care to admit. It has also seeped into every song I have written since the day I met her. Still, if she were to ask me that question, I would answer with insatiable hunger and greed because that answer has always belonged to her.

Instead, I blamed my feelings on nerves and convinced myself it was all part of the process. But as the days until my departure drew closer, it became harder. There was so much I wanted to tell her, but I knew I couldn't (especially after what happened last time). Over time, more was at stake, and I realized I couldn't do that to her. To him. To myself. To the band. To the fans. So, I stayed silent. Instead, I've been sending her cryptic messages through our music. We may perform for crowds, but I've only been playing for her. Sadly, without her knowing, it almost ended. I always thought she'd never hear those lyrics again because I kept them locked away in a vault of my true feelings.

Trust me, it's hard to reach for something—or someone—who won't reach back. I often ask myself why I've been so hung up on the idea that she and I had a chance. I knew I would eventually have to let go, but no one ever explained how painful unrequited love would be. It fucking sucks.

We walk out of my bedroom, where I pause to take her in. The memory of her arms around me quickly fades, like the lies I've told myself over the years: She will see that I am The One. We will end up together. Give it time, and she will choose you.

It was all just lies. If they had been true, something would have happened by now. Or maybe it's my fault because I've stood in my own way enough times to ruin my chances. Either way, it's too late to do anything about it now.

Or is it?

I linger, clutching onto the goodbye as if my life depended on it. I want to ask the question. I want to say those three little words, but I fear it would only echo my voice back to me as if I were screaming into an abyss.

However, it was at that very moment that I realized that no matter how much I loved this girl, holding onto false hope was no good for me. If we were meant to be together, if I truly wanted to be with her, I would have tried harder. I would have let her know. I would have been honest enough so she could make a choice. I have suffered long enough, loving her more than I could ever imagine loving anyone in my entire life. The longing has been like a broken string on my guitar; a lost song from the most beautiful songbird that no one could hear; a dancer who can no longer find their rhythm. It has taken over everything. It was the art of letting go.

I forced a smile, ignoring my screaming heart. As for her, she looked at me with the eyes of someone who cares about a friend.

And nothing more.

My vision clears as I exhale a sigh of relief. Even after regaining consciousness, I am deeply aware of how firmly rooted I am in my past. Just thinking about it makes me uneasy, which is why I seek this closure—why I need it. I have been stuck on this chapter for years, and I believe every story must come to an end.

I drive with the windows down, smelling the scent of freshly cut grass and the evaporating morning dew as it fills my senses. In the distance, I hear the soft sounds of church bells fading into a distant echo. For a moment, I forget how long my journey will be or how long it took me to get here.

Soon, I make a sharp turn onto a side street. My pulse quickens as I see the bus station on the horizon. Already, nerves swarm my body like fire ants I can't swat away fast enough. But I refuse to let anything stop me. Sometimes, in my mind's eye, I see her. Sometimes, I see the two of us. Sometimes, I see much more. Now it's time to figure out how much of it is real.

Chapter Three
Now

My pickup glides smoothly into an empty parking space like a glove. It's an extended cab with a decent-sized bed in the back. Had I not decided to restore it, it would have fallen into disrepair, becoming nothing but a rust bucket on wheels. Something inside me, however, feels oddly attached to it, which is a surprise, considering how I once despised the thing. But no matter how many vehicles I've owned throughout my life, I always seem to be drawn to this truck like a favorite shirt—or a security blanket.

I believe that much of my good fortune in life is due to timing. The magic of serendipitous moments—unexpected events that can't be explained but feel incredibly magical—plays a significant role. When my high school friends and I decided to start a band, our lives ignited with passions we didn't even realize were deep inside us. We were passionate skaters (skateboarders, not those cheesy rollerbladers) who decided to trade our boards for beats, which sparked the beginning of our band's origin story (and another story, but more on that later).

It was a typical Friday night when we all gathered to eat junk food and watch whatever new release we found at Blockbuster that evening. Nothing was worse than browsing the aisle only to find movie cases with nothing behind them. I imagine trying to explain this to today's youth, because in the '90s, we didn't have streaming. If a show was on, you either stayed home to watch it or missed it until the rerun. The idea of streaming was about as far-fetched as a flying car. I could go on, but that's not the point of this story. Still, I'd do anything for a commercial break right now.

"Picture it: Sicily, 1997." I'm joking. But seriously, picture it: Auburn, NY, 1997. The guys and I were hanging out at my house after school since none of us had shifts at the record store in the mall. We were your average teenagers—misfits, honestly. Who decided to drop organized sports to enjoy life without those rules. We ordered two large pizzas and wings for under $30.00, which is a bargain today. Dax picked out *I Know What You Did Last Summer* for us to watch. It was close to Halloween, but we were obviously too old for trick-or-treating, so we went with a scary movie instead. Besides the pizza, Monty brought some candy from his pantry: Razzles and Pop Rocks. This was also when urban legends had us convinced that Pop Rocks and soda were as dangerous as turning on the car's light while driving or swimming right after eating. I could keep going, but again that's not the point here. The only organ that's going to explode in this story is my heart — not my stomach. Did I give anything away?

We were spread out between the floor and the couch, eating junk food and watching trash TV while talking about everything and anything that came to mind. It was then, just before we put in the movie, that Dax announced he had an idea.

"I know you can play guitar." —He looked at me— "And you can write."

Yeah? So what? And I can play drums," Monty added. *"And don't forget Jordan over here. He may suck on a board, but he's sick on the bass."* He points to Jordan, who had a piece of pizza hanging out of his mouth. *"What's your point?"*

"Well, I can sing." Dax practically jumps from his spot on the couch. *"So, I was thinking... We should start a band! It only makes sense!"*

Monty bursts out laughing until he notices the serious expression plastered across Dax's face. "Oh, you're actually being serious?"

"Yes, I'm serious, you ass." Dax throws a pillow at him, knocking the packet of Pop Rocks out of his hand. *"I've actually been putting a lot of thought into this, and I think we could really be something."*

"Do you even know the statistics?" I swallow a gulp of soda. *"Do you know how many bands actually make it? Not many,"* I say.

"What do you want to be, the next Backstreet Boy or something?" Jordan snickers, almost knocking over my mom's bowl of potpourri as he begins humming one of their songs.

"Yeah," Monty joined in with Jordan. Quit Playing Games With My Heart, *he sang as he placed his hand over his chest.*

"Just listen to me for a second, OK? Music is changing. Rock n' Roll is evolving. We're seeing alternative rock become more popular. Not to mention, there will be a shift in what people want to hear, like punk. You've heard Blink-182. I want that," he said without taking a breath. "I want to find our voice. I want us to be cutting-edge, but still mainstream."

"You have about a snowball's chance in hell, my friend." I stood up and patted him on the back as I reached for another slice of pizza.

"Yes, but you can write the music." He looked at me as if I were a beacon of hope. "You took that creative writing class last year, didn't ya? I know you can do it." His eyes bore into mine. "Come on, Luke! Let's at least give this a try. If we don't make it by graduation, you can have the pleasure of telling me you told me so."

"I don't know; it might be fun," Monty shrugs. "Besides skateboarding, we really have nothing else going on." He dumped the remaining Pop Rocks into his mouth.

"Yeah, because we definitely can't skate in the winter," Jordan cut in. "And it will be here before we know it. Plus, you guys know how much my mom hates it when I hang around the house with nothing to do."

"So, does that mean we are doing this?" Dax looks around at us.

"Fine, but only until graduation," I tell him. "That's it. If we don't catch our big break by then, we'll disband—for lack of better words."

"Great!" Dax exclaims. "Now, all we need to do is come up with a name. Any ideas?"

I pull my bag and guitar case out from the backseat of my pickup. I take a deep breath, inhaling the sweet scent of the new day. For a moment, I find peace. I am calm. For once, something about all of this feels right. Could this finally be my time?

My cell phone vibrates in my pocket. I pull it out to see who's calling. Once I do, I take a deep breath and answer. "Hey, dude," I say. "What's up?"

"Just checking to see how you're doing," he pauses, "and also *what* you're doing," the voice on the other end responds.

"Don't play dumb, Monty," I jest. "You know where I am," I respond as I head into the bus station.

"Chill out," he chuckles. "Can't a guy check up on his friend?"

"Well, I'm fine," I say. "You don't need to babysit me."

"I know you are, Luke, but this trip," he hesitates briefly, "I feel like there's so much we need to work out first."

My free hand rubs against my temple, but I don't respond right away. "It still hurts, you know?"

"Your head or your heart?" he asks. But before I can say anything else, he keeps going, "I mean, do you think you're ready for all of this? Do you even understand things well enough?"

"How long do you expect me to wait, Monty? I think I've waited long enough."

"And how long do you think you've waited?" he asks.

"What kind of question is that?"

"Never mind," he says. "I just want you to take it easy. You're only starting to feel better, and I don't think this shock to your system would be good for you."

"What do you know about what is good for me?" I ask.

He sighs. "That's not what I'm trying to say, Luke. But I think we're missing a few steps here. Shouldn't you be prepared first, like, emotionally debrief yourself? I believe you might uncover more than you'd expect…"

"What's that supposed to mean? Are you telling me it's pointless? You know how much I love her, Monty." I can feel the emotional rage building inside me. Out of all people, he should understand how I feel about this. Why is he now being so unsupportive?

"I just don't want to see you crumble. I've seen it happen before for a different reason, and it wasn't very good. You know I've always wanted what's best for you, which is why I feel like we need to talk first," he says.

"Talk about what? The band?" I hold back from yelling. "You are so worried about us getting back together."

"Jeez, Luke. You're so wrong, it's kind of scary," he huffs. "Either way, I can come with you if you want.

"No offense, but we spend enough time together," I grimace.

"Well, I'd be happy to move out," he laughs.

I like to think that I am a man of many thoughts—thoughts that used to find their home on paper, forming my lyrical journal of sorts. It has always been my way of channeling my emotions. Sometimes, I find myself so deep in thought that a pen becomes a makeshift shovel to dig myself out of emotionally sticky situations. But no matter how many words I string together or how perfectly they harmonize with the music from my guitar, they never quite express how I truly feel inside. I guess the pain was always too deep. No song powerful enough to uncover what truly lies beneath the façade I spent years cultivating. Maybe this journey was my swan song of sorts.

And I guess now is a good time, if there is one, to acknowledge the other part of this journey: "The Stoneflower Revolution," which has recently become quite a conspiracy. *Is it real? That's what the fans of Slight Chance want to know!* —was the headline circulating in the media for the past few years. I'm not upset at the person who leaked it (even though I have a good idea who it was), but I chose to keep it to myself until I was ready to reveal its existence to the world. It was never about what it was; it has always been about who it was for.

Yet something about today feels promising. It feels like a weight has been lifted off my shoulders. Every time I attempted this trip before, I was instantly reminded of that one night over twenty years ago when my world came crashing down. It felt the same way I imagine a mountain crumbling would. I always thought that something called "heart-shattering" was just a phrase, but that night, I realized it meant exactly that. Mine shattered beyond repair. The breath escaped my lungs as if I were drowning. And since then, I haven't been able to come up for air.

I stepped out of my truck holding a bouquet of pink peonies (her favorite) in one hand while gripping the leather-bound journal tightly in the other. I walked up the driveway, rehearsing everything I wanted to say that I had kept locked in my heart's vault for years. Finally, my moment had arrived. I was ready to pour it all out. I had nothing to lose.

Or so I thought.

As I approached her house, I looked through the living room window and saw a small child playing with a toy on the floor. I remember it was a toy truck, but it might have also been a train, a car, or even a doll. A cartoon was on the TV, which was centered above the fireplace. Was someone visiting? I wasn't sure.

I was just a few feet from her front door when I saw him. So much happened in those brief seconds that it felt like a tornado of events, making it hard to focus on just one thing. All my feelings flew around like emotional debris. My breath hitched as her face finally came into focus. All I knew for sure was that destruction was imminent, and the first to go was my heart.

The flowers in my hand had fallen onto the porch, petals scattering around my feet. The sky darkened; it felt almost ominous—purely for emotional effect. The day was ending, and I couldn't help but see it as a sign. It was the end. So, I quickly turned around and headed back to my truck. Once inside, I immediately rolled down the windows and tossed the journal onto the passenger seat. I felt like I was suffocating. I wanted to tear my shirt off. I tried to rip off my seatbelt and escape my skin. I stuck my face out the window, inhaling deep breaths and slowly exhaling into the night air.

I wanted to burn that journal and all the memories it held. But I knew that even if I turned it into ashes, nothing is strong enough to destroy the memories attached to it.

Even now, that memory still has the power to stop me in my tracks. It freezes me in place. It lingers in the background of my life, burning in my heart. It keeps replaying in my mind like a broken record.

I don't remember how long I sat in my truck, but everything she and I shared flashed before my eyes, like they say happens right before you die. All the memories. All the feelings. All the words spoken and left unsaid, clenched in the pit of my stomach with no way out. In that moment, I truly felt that the vision I had of us had died, which would never rest in peace.

How foolish I was to think I could come back, and everything would be perfect. That even though time had passed, the feelings between us wouldn't have changed. It was just a break, after all.

Right?

Chapter Four
Now

My nerves have always been of the shaken, not stirred, variety. They tend to be jumbled and nonsensical until they're fully strained. I think that's why I've always been a good writer (well, songwriter, that is). Communicating my feelings in any other way never worked well for me. But as soon as I put pen to paper, I could express myself better than spoken words ever could.

Over the years, as I have refined my craft, I have lived for the lines that flood my heart with emotion. As a lover of music, I find the power it holds to evoke feelings ranging from sadness to happiness, or something in between, truly remarkable. Even transcending. And the pride I feel from creating a lyrical masterpiece is unmatched by anything else. Well, almost anything else.

Writing the perfect lyrics and pairing them with the perfect melody is truly the chef's kiss—or a rockstar's. Sometimes, something as simple as a tune, a key change, or even the range for which a line is sung can create a kind of magic that can be felt in parts of you that you never knew existed. These are the moments I live for.

After checking in at the ticket counter, I found an empty seat in the waiting area. This has always been the part of the journey that affects me the most: waiting. I know what they say about idle hands. It's almost the same as having an idle mind. Instead of keeping my hands busy, my mind tends to fill the time with reasons why I shouldn't be here. Confusion takes over, and suddenly I can't tell what I'm sure of. My mind has a knack for generating doubts. But today, I'm holding onto the one good reason why I should.

Some people might find it embarrassing to have held onto feelings for someone this long. However, I believe it's admirable to keep the flame burning. It's easy for the winds of change to blow it out, but when you love something deeply, you do everything you can to protect it. Not even a flicker. Not one.

I scan the terminal before reaching into my bag to find my journal. After all these years, the leather has become bruised, tarnished, and wrinkled like an old chair. I pull it out and quickly flip through a few pages, noticing the finger smudges in the corners.

Man, if this journal could talk... It's been a part of me longer than I want to admit. Even though it's never had its moment in the spotlight, I'm finally ready to open it up—like my heart—and share it with the world.

The sun shines brightly through the station windows, causing my eyes to strain. It feels intense this morning, almost impossible to see clearly. The words on the pages start to blur, much like my confidence in this journey. Still, I keep going. I hold the journal in my hands as if it's a rare artifact. To some, it might seem that way. I know many journalists and music executives have regarded it as a mythical story—hearing about its existence but never actually seeing it with their own eyes, as if it were the Loch Ness Monster or the Holy Grail.

After our band broke up—or took a break, depending on whether you ask Ross or Rachel—I decided to stay under the radar as much as possible. I was tired of getting questions about the rumors swirling around why things ended the way they did. I knew that put pressure on the guys, which wasn't fair, but I had no choice but to lay low for a while.

From what I was told, Jordan played in a few other bands, while Dax tried his hand at a solo career. Monty, however, was too shattered after the breakup to move on. As for me, I enjoyed the quiet. I was surprisingly content with the break. I didn't have an anxious need to play any music for quite some time. But out of nowhere, like sugar on a tongue, I had a taste of it again and felt the desire for music seep back in with unstoppable force.

Just as I was about to open my journal for some lyrical escape, a young kid plopped down across from me. But I was so wrapped up in the struggle with the sun and my thoughts that I barely noticed. It wasn't until his red backpack hit the ground that I realized he was there.

I noticed he was wearing a faded black t-shirt with an unfamiliar logo stretched across his chest. I tried making out what the logo meant, but my attention shifted to the tattoo peeking out from his sleeve instead. It made me remember my first tattoo and how I never stopped to think about what it was or what it symbolized. Back then, I only cared that I was getting one. Now, it's just a reminder of a time when I was clueless. Everything I've collected since then means more to me.

"Good morning," I say.

The young man—or kid, considering our obvious age gap— nods back at me while barely glancing up from his phone. His movement causes his dirty blonde hair, which hangs over his face, to flap into the air, revealing his half-lidded green eyes hidden behind it. His expression gives me emo throwback vibes, but I'm almost sure he'd ignore me completely if I told him that. Then again, he hardly makes eye contact with me as it is, which eventually makes my smile fade.

A sour expression tightens his face, with the corners of his mouth hanging almost as far as his sharp jaw, as if someone had painted them on for dramatic effect. Right away, I want to know his story.

"I feel like you almost have to wear sunglasses in here," I chuckle. "I just don't want to be that person, ya know?" I say, hoping he'll notice me this time. Instead, he stays glued to his phone.

His posture is terrible. His body slouches further into his seat the longer I watch him. But I was no different at that age. Yet, here I am, judging him the same way I was once judged. It's funny how that works. We forget what it was like—but not me. Not really.

Suddenly, he looks up and nods at my guitar. "You play?"

"No, I carry it around for exercise," I joke. "Kidding. Yes, I play. You?"

The kid nods again as he reaches into his bag, pulling out a pair of drumsticks. "Drums." He holds them out as if I needed a visual reference.

"Are you any good?" I ask.

"Are *you*?" he shoots back.

I can't help but laugh. His sarcasm is oddly comforting. "I've been told I am—or was," I finally say.

"What do you mean by that?" His eyes squint toward me.

"Back in my heyday, I was good. But I haven't played professionally in quite some time. For a while, I just played solo to satisfy that creative outlet," I explain. "Are you in a band?"

"Yeah." He quickly points to the logo on his shirt. "This is my band," he says with a smile that spreads across his face like wildfire.

"The…" I try to make out the words, but they are too faded to decipher.

"The Illusionists," he interrupts, running his finger over the faded letters. "Have you ever heard of us?"

"The Illusionists? You sound like a bunch of magicians," I laugh.

"That's what I said!" he exclaims, slapping his knee. "But the guys never listen to me."

"I can relate. That's just how some bands speak, I'm afraid. Too many cooks in the kitchen," I say.

"So, what do you do about it then?" His posture stiffens like an obedient student.

"Well," I clear my throat, "you have to listen to each other; otherwise, you're doomed."

He nods as if he's considering what I said. "I'm Robbie, by the way."

"Luke." I reach for his hand, which he holds longer than I expected, as if searching for something, but then he quickly pulls away when his eyes meet mine.

"What about your band? Are you still together?" he asks.

Well, now that's a complicated question (kind of like everything else in my life right now). I don't think we are broken up, nor are we officially together at the moment. We're in a gray area without a clear label. Maybe I should have taken Monty up on his offer to explain why that is. There's a gap in my timeline I can't quite figure out. But I can't tell this kid all of that.

"So, where are you headed, kid?" I shifted the subject away from his question.

"Home," he answers. "You?"

Home, too," I say.

"I would have driven home, but my car was taken from me," he says, rolling his eyes as if I'm personally responsible. "I was out here for a show with the band, and now I'm heading back." His voice trails off.

"Where are they now?" I ask.

"Who?" He narrows his eyes.

"Your bandmates." I hide a chuckle.

"Oh." He brushes his hair back from his face. "We got into an argument, and I left."

"Sorry, kid. That's tough."

"You have no idea," he mumbles under his breath. "It's just that our lead singer, Garrett, is a real pain in the ass. He thinks he *is* the band and the rest of us are just stage decorations." He crosses his arms over his chest.

"Well, how do the other guys feel about that?" I ask.

"The same. But I'm the only one brave enough to say anything." He slouches.

"I'm sure everything will work out in the end," I offer, aware that many bands die on this very hill. "So, why was your car taken away?"

"You don't know?" He looks at me.

"No. You didn't tell me," I say.

"Oh." He shakes his head. "Dropped out of college. It's like everyone is always trying to make me into something I'm not. I mean, they get to do what they want. Why can't I?"

I smile. He sounds just like me once upon a time.

"What's so funny?" His face twists.

"I'm just very familiar with the feeling, that's all. Why did you drop out?"

"I didn't see myself working some pencil-pushing job after I graduated, *pfft*," Robbie continues, blowing air through his lips. "It's just not me. It's not what I want to do. So, I figured I was doing everyone a favor by not wasting thousands of dollars on school."

"Let me guess, you think you're going to make it big?" I raised my eyebrows in question.

"Here we go again." He sits up taller only to slouch back down. "Let me guess, you think I'm chasing an impossible dream or wasting my time on a band that probably won't make it anywhere?" He rolls his eyes in an attempt to mock me.

"Hey, now. You're talking to a fellow musician here," I said, raising my hands defensively. "So, you want to play drums professionally? Be the next Travis Barker?"

"Who's that?" he asks.

"Are you kidding me?!" I almost fall out of my seat. "You don't know who Travis Barker is?"

He shakes his head.

"What about Matt Cameron, Lars Ulrich, Taylor Hawkins, Tré Cool, Dave Grohl?!" I hold my hand to my heart, worried that this kid was about to crush it.

"Oh, yeah, the Nirvana guy. My dad is a huge fan of them," he says.

"Your dad is smart. They were instrumental in shaping the '90s music scene."

"I actually want to be a songwriter as well," he offers.

"That's incredible. I think you and I have a lot in common, kid." I lean back in my seat.

"If that's the case, got any advice on how to deal with writer's block? It just sucks because it all started after I quit school. It's almost as if the universe doesn't want me to succeed—like I'm being punished or something." His hand wipes the small beads of sweat from his forehead before casually transferring the remnants onto his bag. The sun and lack of proper ventilation are showing no mercy.

"The words will find you, trust me. You need to give it time," I say.

"Do you still write?"

"Not so much anymore." I tap my finger on the leather-bound journal in my lap. The back is decorated with infamous '90s smiley faces, a yin-yang, and a few band stickers, all of which have faded and peeled over time. The front, however, features a flower etched in the center.

"Is that it?" he asks. "Your songwriting book, that is."

I nodded just as the announcer called out my bus number which we both stood up for at the exact same time.

"Looks like we are headed in the same direction. Mind if I sit near you?" he asks as we make our way toward the bus.

"Sure, kid."

"And could I read some of your songs?"

"You want to read my songs?" I turn back to face him as he shrugs as if it's no big deal. "I wouldn't want you to run off with them, being an illusionist and all," I smirk.

"I promise not to steal them," he raises his hand in defense. "Just looking for some helpful inspiration."

After we take our seats on the bus, Robbie tells me he needs to make a quick call home. He turns away, holding his phone against his ear while I prepare for someone to read my work. It's been years since I've let anyone get close to this book. Still, it would be nice to get an opinion from a fellow musician.

I try not to eavesdrop, but it's hard to ignore his bobbing head, as if the person on the other end could see him.

"Yeah, well, so far, so good," he says as he turns to face me. "So far, so good." He smiles.

Chapter Five
Now

Writing comes from a place of emotion. It can stem from something fleeting or from something much deeper. It's the difference between lowercase and uppercase emotions. You can express them differently through tone and inflection. Sometimes, it's not even about what you say; it's how you say it.

Today feels like lowercase emotions—a ripple beneath the surface of the creek, a gentle tremor. It's a gust of wind strong enough to tousle your hair but not enough to uproot trees.

I settle into my seat after putting my bag in the overhead compartment. Robbie is next to me, playing with his phone, just as two loud bangs echo through the air. We all watch as the driver yanks the key hard in the ignition before slamming his hand on the steering wheel in frustration. A few minutes later, he tries again, and we watch anxiously from our seats. Then, we hear another couple of loud bangs as he turns the key in the ignition again. This time, he doesn't hit the steering wheel in defeat; instead, he shakes his head.

"Blasted thing," he says just as a small cloud of smoke billows up from the hood.

"That doesn't look good," Robbie points out.

I slump into my seat. This was the first time I had made it this far, and as luck would have it, the damn bus won't start. Go figure.

"Folks," the driver says over the intercom, "looks like we aren't going anywhere anytime soon. I apologize, but you will need to take your belongings and return to the station."

Passengers immediately start huffing and complaining as they gather their things and storm off the bus. I couldn't believe what was happening. All I could do was laugh at the irony of it all.

"What now?" Robbie looks at me as if I were his keeper.

"Not sure, kid," I shrug. "It doesn't look like we're leaving anytime soon."

"You drove here, right?" He looks at me expectantly. "We can drive?"

"You mean, I can drive?" I laughed as I considered this idea. It wasn't part of my original plan, but then again, when has anything ever gone as planned for me? "Fine," I agree. "But I'll need to stop home first to get some provisions. We might as well head back to my place and clear out the pantry."

My truck slows as it pulls up to the curb of my spacious Victorian home. It features white board and batten siding, black shutters, and black double doors with an antique brass knocker, blending modern and vintage charm. The house has been worth every penny I've spent on it. Still, no one would guess it's home to a former rock star. Then again, I don't really fit the part of a former rock star either. Should I be living in the Hollywood Hills? Nah. That's not me.

"Home sweet home," Robbie says, his eyes widening as he takes it all in while the metal gate opens after I enter the security code.

"Yep, home sweet home," I repeat just as the gates close behind my truck.

"You didn't say you made it *that* big," he says. "Do you live alone?"

"Afraid not."

"I was going to say that it seems like a big house for just one person," he says as we step out of my truck.

"I live with a roommate," I say while shutting the door behind me. "We have been friends since high school."

We leave our bags as we walk up my freshly mowed lawn and the few wooden steps to my house. The porch, which was updated a few years after I moved in, wraps around the entire house and extends into a large gathering area in the back. From there, I extended the roofline to add twinkling lights, creating a sense of romance and peace. Often, I turn them on and sit outside with my guitar. Visions of happier times, with smiling faces and music filling the space, echo through the emptiness inside my heart.

After punching in the house's security code, I push open the door, feeling an immediate sense of pride as Robbie takes in my home. We step into the foyer, where a small round table greets us.

I was once told by an interior designer that most homes of this size have them for aesthetic purposes, but I find it's nothing more than a great place to store my mail and keys (as does Monty).

"Whoa," Robbie gasps as he walks toward the small sitting room off the foyer, where he notices all my posters and records decorating the walls. It's less of a sitting room than a shrine to my past. It's a place I go to pray and thank the Rock Gods for giving me such a good career, no matter how short-lived it was. If music is my religion, then this would be my temple.

As I follow behind him, the floorboards creak beneath our feet as my fingers glide smoothly along the shiny surface of the chair rail. I guide it around the room until I reach the leather sofa, where I take a seat while Robbie continues exploring. He walks around the room as if it were a museum, learning about ancient artifacts. I don't mind. It's nice to see someone interested in my past (or, at least, a part of it).

"How long ago did you build this house?" he asks.

"A long time ago. It surprised me that I—" I cut myself off as he kept moving through the room.

"I still can't believe you're Luke from Slight Chance," he almost whispers, his voice catching. "Do you understand that you're Luke from Slight Chance?"

"Oh, yeah, the posters," I say, realizing how he made the connection.

"They were among the biggest bands of the late 90s and early 2000s. What happened?"

"Same thing that happens with most bands," I answer. "The more fame, the more conflict. We had a lot of strong, stubborn personalities that got in the way of the music, but I think we could have survived it." My voice trails off.

Robbie approaches my desk and sees a magazine open to an article featuring a picture of my face: *Lucas "Luke" Grant's agent from the notorious '90s emo band Slight Chance, made a statement yesterday that the artist who has been away from the music scene for a while is considering reuniting with his former bandmates. If this happens, the band plans to release their fourth studio album. Fans can't wait. But they also want to know, is he ready?*

"Wait a minute," Robbie looks up at me— "You're back?"

"Being back is a loose term in the music industry, kid. You never know how people will perceive your 'comeback.' But yeah, I figured why not give it another shot, ya know?"

"So, you made up your mind then? You're going to reunite with them?" His eyebrows lift until they are hidden beneath the hair hanging over his forehead.

"More or less," I say. "There are just a few things I need to figure out first."

"He's just being difficult," Monty says as he peeks his head around the corner.

"Look who it is!" Robbie shouts as if he's about to reunite with an old friend, but quickly corrects himself. "It's Monty Tennison! That's Monty Tennison!" he exclaims as if I didn't know. "You didn't tell me your roommate was Monty!" Robbie's eyes practically pop out of his head. "This is turning out better than I ever expected."

"What is?" I ask.

"Oh," Robbie steps back. "This whole journey back home. Can I take a picture?" He pulls out his phone. "I want to remember this day forever."

"Well, say 'cheese,' Monty," I smirk.

"Oh, no, pretty boy, you're in the picture, too." He yanks me off the leather couch.

After he snaps a picture and a selfie with us three, he asks, "So, what makes you guys want to reunite? Why now?" Robbie looks toward Monty, who has a more open expression.

"It's a long story," he deadpans.

"I just don't understand," Robbie continues, "Why keep this from me?"

"Well, I wouldn't exactly say I was keeping anything from you," I say. "We just met, kid." But he's not even listening to me. Instead, he walks out of the room and takes himself on a private tour of my home, leaving the conversation and the room behind. I don't mind. Kids are curious creatures.

Next to the shrine of my past is a much larger living room that looks like it was straight out of an interior design magazine. I honestly don't remember making these design choices, but I'm not upset about it either. Nothing seems out of place—or actually lived in. The pillows are perfectly fluffed with what I call a nice karate chop in the middle. Off that room is a large kitchen with marble countertops. The island is huge, meant to serve as a favorite gathering spot. There's even a small breakfast nook with banquet seating and a refinished table tucked away in the corner. It's a table from my childhood—a symbol of new beginnings.

Upstairs, there are five bedrooms and three bathrooms, not counting the small bathroom on the main floor and the guest bathroom in the basement. The house is perfect, except for how lonely it sometimes makes me feel. But to be fair, Monty has been keeping me company for reasons I don't understand. His reasons often change whenever I ask him how long he plans to stay. I originally bought this place as a surprise for her. It had so much charm and character that I could easily picture us raising a family here. But as soon as Robbie makes his presence known again, I am reminded of my familiar loneliness. It's crazy to think I could have easily had a son about his age by now. Funny how plans work out. Life certainly didn't give two shits about mine.

"This house is amazing," Robbie says as he drops into one of the counter stools.

"That it is," Monty agrees.

"You probably have good acoustics, given how empty it is," Robbie continues, unaware of how his words impact me. Loneliness often reflects your sorrows back to you.

"You know what I think, kid?" Monty plops down on the stool next to him. "There is one room in this house I think you would absolutely love," Monty says as he peers over at me, and instantly, I know what room he is referring to.

Robbie asks, "What room is that?"

"First, do you play?" Monty asks, turning to face him.

"He is an illusionist," I tease.

"A what?" Monty's face scrunches.

"It's my band's stupid name," Robbie huffs. "But I'm not too bad. Genetics saved me there." He winks as if it's some inside joke he has yet to let me in on. "My dad can play—and sing."

"Say no more. Follow me," Monty says as he hops up from his seat and leads him toward the basement door.

"You're not going to kill me down here, are you?" Robbie asks as he looks back at me just as I turn on the light.

Monty chuckles. "Only one way to find out." He waves his hands in a spooky manner.

We head down into the basement, past the small home theater and bar area, until we stop in front of a set of doors. "After you." Monty gestures for Robbie to go ahead as I turn on another light, revealing the infamous room: the studio.

"Holy shit," Robbie exclaims, jumping up and down as if he just won the lottery. "This is so freakin' cool!"

I grab an extra guitar of mine and lead him toward the booth where Monty is already setting up his drums.

"Are we really going to play?" Tears shimmer in his eyes, which he quickly wipes away. "Are we?"

"That's the plan." I smile. "What should we play first?"

"I don't care. We could play 'Row, Row, Row Your Boat,' and I wouldn't care," Robbie affirms.

"How about we take a trip down memory lane, eh?" Monty looks at me. "You up for it, Luke?"

"How far are we traveling?" I chuckle.

"Leather journal far?" he cocks his head at me.

"Wait," Robbie interrupts. "Is this the leather journal you had at the bus station with the flower etched on the cover?"

"You've seen it?" Monty's eyes widen before turning back to face me.

Robbie nods his head. "Can we play one of those songs?"

I turned away, but I don't know for how long. What my agent never told the journalist (nor did I tell my agent, for that matter) was that the main goal of this reunion was to end my career with the album it should have started with. I want the chance to release the music I wrote when the words felt forbidden. Yet, they were the most authentic. They were passionate. They were raw. They were every bit of my heart on paper. Unfortunately, I don't blame anyone for how things turned out. I probably would have reacted the same way. I'm just hoping that, over time, the emotional climate between us and this journal has changed.

Outside of this journal, I remember the first song I ever wrote. I was sitting at the edge of the lake. The pier was empty, except for a few young kids fishing. They cast their lines into the water, waiting for something to happen. But for the longest time, nothing did, much like my writing back then.

My eyes were fixed on the water. I stared into it, hoping for some kind of inspiration to wash ashore or maybe for one of the kids to catch something worth writing about. But neither happened. No matter how long I looked into the water or at the greenery around me, the words wouldn't come. I'm no stranger to that feeling; I've been there many times before. It saddened me to think that writer's block isn't something you defeat once and never face again.

Still, I pushed myself to go back to the lake day after day as the autumn leaves prepared for the upcoming snow. Lazily, I started the engine and drove away. My face was like stone, not moving a single muscle as I made the trip like a robot on autopilot. At that moment, I forgot what it was like to feel the corners of my mouth turn upward into a hopeful smile. It was as if every ounce of optimism had completely disappeared within me; my face was as vacant as my soul felt. I was once again confronting the truth about how I felt at the time: empty and without faith.

It was during my third week that I returned to the lake, feeling like I was hanging on the edge of my creative rope. That's when I realized those were the feelings I needed to draw from. If I wanted to be vulnerable and transparent, what better way than to express the very core of my soul? But what was in my soul? What needed to be released? That was still a mystery. And just as the autumn weather was fading toward winter, I let it all go. It was time.

When my eyes refocused, I saw an older man fishing alone. He cast his line into the water and settled into his lawn chair, waiting patiently for a bite. He was wrapped in a flannel blanket to stay warm.

All of a sudden, he jumped from his seat as he felt a tug on his line. The blanket flew into the air before landing in a flannel puddle on the pier. He wound the line back, and to his amazement, a small fish hung from the other end. In the world of fishing (where I am clearly no expert), the fish didn't look that impressive. But to him, it was. It was all down to perspective. That could have been his greatest catch to date, which made me realize that it wasn't about how others viewed our achievements, but how we personally viewed them.

Getting back to the present, Monty and Robbie are both looking at me as if I had been lost for quite some time. What's there to say? But to open that journal and play one of my songs? I wasn't sure. It felt too risky. Too soon—like removing a bandage before the wound was healed.

Yet, somehow, breaking through the barrier of heartbreak, the songs reminded me of simpler times. Just the thought of hearing them again would bring me closer to the pulse of my music—to her.

Then again, I've always been a sucker for a bit of nostalgia, especially since the journal was still inside the backpack I'd had since high school.

So, I guess, without further ado, let's rock out like it's 1997.

Admit
One
Get Ready to
Party
Like it's 1997

Chapter Six
1997

I don't pretend to know a lot. In fact, I find the imagination to be a frightening thing at times, especially when I'm lost in a world of melodies that take my lyrics to places my conscious mind wouldn't dare to go. At best, I use my imagination carefully, under the guidance of a notebook, a pen, and the need to evoke emotion. Lately, I've experienced what most would call writer's block. However, I find that term unsatisfactory and somewhat lacking in substance. It's more like an "I-am-going-to-kill-your-dream-and-everything-you-hoped-for-in-your-life-block."

Personally, I believe that a setback this big should carry a lot more weight, as it can threaten a person's life purpose and those of my three friends, who depend on my guitar and writing skills for us to succeed as a band. But as I lie in bed tonight, I instantly feel the suffocating pressure take hold of me. Now I understand what it's like to be a prisoner to your craft.

Bands aren't what they used to be. There's a change in the wind—a shift—that's bringing a new sound. I believe that after we enter the new millennium, this will steer music in a direction none of us expect. I can't bring myself to take down my Nirvana posters from my wall because even though I haven't made it in the music scene, they remind me to stay humble, knowing Kurt Cobain was never someone to sell out. Fame isn't everything and would never be my main goal. Music is simply a creative outlet for self-expression. Still, when the lights go out, it feels *more* dangerous.

Pop music seems to be popping (for lack of a better word). Boy bands are pulling at the heartstrings of every girl in the foreseeable future, while girl groups are trendy. And since I have no desire to "Spice Up My Life" or "MMMBop" my way into the scene, I am sticking with what I know.

I find words to be funny. I say this because I use them every day. They escape from my lips and float around inside my head like dandelions in the wind. However, those slippery little suckers leave me whenever I try to make them permanent in this world. They dangle in front of me teasingly, and when I try to grab hold of them, they fly away, never to return. Words are funny that way. Dax, my best friend and the one who apparently has no fear of singing in front of a crowd, could probably sing my lyrics better than I could ever dream of doing myself.

During a trial run to evaluate our talent, Dax performed a few cheesy poems I had written for a creative writing project the previous year. Hearing the words I once thought meaningful now strikes the ears with a mix of immaturity and amateurishness. Still, there was a certain conviction in the way the words came from his mouth. It was as if he wrote them—he felt them—and now he was sharing those feelings with the world. Lead singers naturally assume ownership of their band's songs (whether they wrote them or not). It's the perception that matters, which has little to do with reality. Yet, we still buy into it, don't we?

Regardless, I have been tasked with creating music for our nameless band. I don't think the guys understand how the writing process works—especially for someone who isn't skilled in the art of songwriting. I'm not angry about this. I'm sad. I'm disappointed that it might take months to write a song that's only two to three minutes long. However, I refuse to rush the process because every time I have tried, the words end up weak and unfulfilling. Even Dax would struggle to back them with convincing emotion. Now, I have nothing. No words come to me. I am lost in a sea of inspiration, with no lifeboats of an idea on the horizon.

Yet, here I am, whispering these thoughts to the ceiling. I count how many times the fan spins above my head. I count how many times I toss and turn, and then, when I think my mind is finally at peace, I count the days that have come and gone. They are the days I can never get back. All I need is time. All I need is inspiration. And if at all possible, the combination of the two. I'm supposed to have at least five songs ready for the band to start rehearsing, and I have zero. Z-E-R-O. Perhaps I should count sheep next.

Still, I dare not look at the alarm clock on my bedside table. I know morning is coming, and the thought of getting up for school makes staying in bed, lost in my worries, seem more relaxing by comparison. I pull the covers up to my chin and roll my pillow into a ball. As the night sky fades into the brightening colors of the rising sun, I do my best to resist the pull. I will deny the sun's existence, and maybe through that denial, I can delay the morning until I am ready to start the day. Wishful thinking, I know. But I unfortunately have nothing to look forward to when I "wake up."

My eyes are closed now. I hide behind the darkness of my eyelids, trying to escape the reality of my situation. But the sun stretches out its long arms, forcing my eyes open just as my alarm clock starts ringing. Morning has arrived, and I feel like I never slept at all. It's one thing to pull an all-nighter when you're working on something important; it's another to do it after wallowing in your sorrows all night.

My face presses firmly against my pillow as the sides swell up and surround my head. I can't breathe when I lie like this, but strangely, suffocation feels like a better option than getting up and facing my writing setbacks.

Wilson, our Golden Retriever, rolls onto his back and stretches across my bed, seemingly unaware of the struggles that troubled me throughout the night. We adopted him from the local animal shelter after he peeked over the fence, reminding me of Wilson from *Home Improvement*. Instantly, I knew he was our dog, and I'm still amazed anyone could have had the heart to give him up. Luckily, we found him. I can't imagine life without him.

I greet Wilson with a pat on his head as I climb out of bed. The blankets slip away from beneath me as I almost roll onto the floor. Almost instantly, the exhaustion from lack of sleep hits me as my tired legs sluggishly drag across my bedroom floor toward the bathroom.

The cold tile greets my feet as I stand up to turn on the shower. The hot water begins to steam up the bathroom like a makeshift sauna, which offers no help in waking me. In fact, it does quite the opposite as I stand under the faucet, feeling as though I could stay like this forever and be fine. I entertain the idea of missing school so I can spend the day napping instead. But I talk myself out of it since my guidance counselor has been on my case lately. So, I refuse to give him any ammunition in the fight.

Eventually, I turn off the shower and reach around the curtain for a towel, but just as I bring it toward me and start drying off, I hear my stepdad, Frank, brushing his teeth. I'm surprised to see he's almost ready to leave for work.

"How long have I been in here?" I yawn as I peek my head out from behind the shower curtain.

"Long enough. I couldn't wait any longer to get in here, I'm afraid," he says before spitting his toothpaste into the sink. "Otherwise, I'd be late for work, just like you're going to be for school." He glances at his watch. "Long night?"

"You could say that." I yawned again, keeping my mouth open as if I'm trying to swallow all the bathroom air.

Silence has become a friend of mine. I spend a lot of time with it at home. Sometimes, it feels quite comforting, but other times, it can feel awkward, like I'm being forced to hang out with someone

I have nothing in common with. I once told my mother that our house felt too quiet, and she responded that most of her life felt too loud. Now, she treasures the quiet. It's a gift she never thought she'd receive. Maybe I need a shift in perspective.

After I get dressed, I walk down the stairs and into the kitchen. Half of the pot of coffee remains, so I quickly pour myself a cup and sit down at the kitchen table. The table can comfortably seat about four people, but it's in very poor shape. It was the first piece of furniture my mother bought after my biological father left us out of the blue. It became a symbol of new beginnings for us. She gained her independence that day when she bought it and loaded it into our pickup without any help from him.

I remember the day as if it were yesterday. He had been traveling a lot for work and was hardly home for school events, dinner, or even the weekends. My mom would constantly ask him to slow down and spend more time with the family, but he would always tell her that he had to work to make ends meet (as if she were the root cause of their financial problems). Even now, I know there's no way a job could pull someone away from their family that often unless they choose to let it. And he made that choice repeatedly. Even when he was home, he was never really present. He was always distracted by something else, which forced us to compete for his attention — and we never won. It was exhausting. So, I stopped asking him to come to my games, and my mom stopped asking if he would be home for dinner. It was much easier to accept his absence than to keep asking for his attendance. An empty spot at the table is easier to deal with when you don't expect someone to fill it.

The week leading up to his official departure, something felt different. The air was heavy. It rested on our shoulders, and no matter how hard you tried to move around it, you crashed into it like a wall. On the day of, I heard my parents arguing in their bedroom, which wasn't anything new per se. The only difference was that it was accompanied by the sounds of drawers opening and closing. I heard my mother crying. I heard the desperation in her voice, pleading for answers that only seemed to hurt her more as she received them. *Why did he carry on like this? Why did he lie for so long? Why would he punish the family he claimed to love?* The questions looped in my mind until I memorized them as my own.

I stood in the hallway, eavesdropping on a conversation, my ears were too young to understand. It wasn't until my dad opened the bedroom door with a bag in his hand that I understand everything. He was leaving again. And this time, he wasn't coming back.

"You won't be home for dinner tonight?" I asked.

His eyes widened. "No, Luke. I won't."

"And you won't be at my game this Saturday, either, huh?"

He looked down at the bag in his hand. "No, son. I won't."

I nodded my head as if I understood what it all meant. However, unaware of the impact of my words, I said, "So, nothing will change."

He bent down to meet my eyes as if to soften whatever blow he was about to deliver, but I spared him the effort. It was too exhausting to keep begging him to be there—to want him to be there.

"Mom and I will be fine," I said. "We've always been fine. You should go."

He stood up, looking at me as if I had just spoken back to him. My mom was in the doorway; her face was red and tear-streaked. She said nothing, as if I had expressed everything she couldn't.

My mother hates that I drink coffee, saying it will stunt my growth, but I'm almost six feet tall, so I don't see how much more growth I needed. The clock on the wall ticks away, reminding me I have exactly twenty minutes before I need to leave for school. But I need this cup—maybe even two. Since Frank usually takes all the travel mugs and leaves them at his office, I have no choice but to drink my coffee here. The last thing I want is hot coffee spilling all over my lap.

I hesitate to try writing again. Even with ten minutes left, I decide to pour myself another cup and open my notebook. My hands hover over the blank pages as if trying to summon words. I close my eyes, trying to think of something to write. But I closed my eyes a little too long, and before I knew it, I woke up three hours later to a spilled cup of coffee and a blank page in my notebook.

"Shit!" I yell as I jump up from my seat at the table. I look over to see our answering machine blinking rapidly. I quickly listen to the messages. They are all from Dax.

"Where are you?" he asked in his first message. "I'm calling you from the school payphone. I only have one quarter left, so you'd better answer if I call again."

The second message came an hour later. "Luke, this isn't funny. You'd better not bail on us tonight. So, bring the music." He slams the phone back onto the receiver.

I couldn't believe I had fallen asleep. I walk over to the dish towel in the sink and start cleaning up my mess. The puddle of coffee is now cold and has mostly stained the cover and edges of my Composition notebook, which was decorated with various stickers I had collected from the local roller dome, where the guys and I used to hang out and meet girls.

I shake off any remaining droplets. Then, I crumple the dish towel into a ball and toss it back into the sink. There is no point even trying to go to school. I'd be useless. I'm too tired. I'm already really late. Whatever energy I got from that unexpected nap, hopefully, is enough to at least recharge my motivation to write.

Since the guys and I decided to form a band, they gave me two lousy weeks to come up with a song. They were eager to start rehearsing, but the pressure of it all has been too much for my feeble writing hands to handle. Nothing came to mind (nothing worth singing about, at least). And every time I saw them, it was all they talked about—all they cared about. It was no longer, "Hey, Luke, how are you doing?" but more like, "Hey Luke, have you written any songs lately?"

So, I decided that for the rest of the day, I would curl up on the couch with my notebook. Wilson stays beside me, casually throwing disapproving looks as if he's aware that I have skipped school, even though he looks exhausted. He rests his golden head in my lap as I pet his silky coat.

I turn on the TV, surprised at how much I miss daytime shows. The marathon of random talk shows and sitcom reruns feels like a treat. I enjoy a few minutes of *Jerry Springer* before I end up falling back asleep to *Ricki Lake* for the rest of the afternoon.

I wake up again when I hear a car door slam. I check the time. It's almost 4:00 pm, which means my mom is home from work. *Shit.* I have exactly 45 minutes until I need to meet the guys at the mall (as long as my mom hasn't found out I played hooky).

"Hey, honey," Mom says as soon as she comes inside. She finds me on the couch. "Are you sick?" She hangs up her coat and takes her shoes off by the door. There's a front closet, but it's packed to the brim with random things, so its original use as a coat closet has become nonexistent. Our shoes and coats are scattered across the entryway like little landmines you have to step over.

I shake my head. "Just a long day. I'm getting up soon, though. I have to meet the guys down at the mall tonight," I painfully lie.

"Oh, do you have to work tonight?" she asks.

"No, it's for a band meeting. I don't have to work until Saturday."

She nods as if trying to recall my schedule, then gazes out the window toward the neighbor's house, which is for sale. "Donna across the street told me that an offer was accepted a few weeks ago. It looks like we'll have new neighbors soon."

"Hopefully, they aren't as terrible," I laugh. But seriously, the couple who lived there before started a neighborhood club where they believed they ran everything and everyone in our small cul-de-sac. Some neighbors followed their ideas and rules, while others, like my family, chose to ignore them. My stepdad would often argue with them about how he maintained our lawn, as if we never mowed or decorated it with pink flamingoes. Eventually, they put their house on the market and moved to a subdivision that better suited their taste — a taste of HOAs and "No Stepping on Lawn" signs.

"How is your writing coming along?" She notices my notebook on the couch.

"It's going," I sigh.

She sits down beside me as Wilson jumps off the couch to make room. "You don't need to put this much pressure on yourself." She pats my knee. "You're too young to be this stressed."

I frown. "Easier said than done, Mom."

"The words will come to you. You just need to feel something first."

Chapter Seven
1997

I park near the JCPenney's department store entrance and head into the mall. I have to dodge countless racks, which seem to pop up every few seconds like I'm playing a strange game of Whac-a-Mole. The mall features three giant fountains—two at each end and one in the center. The central fountain is the largest and holds more pennies than the other two combined. Maybe people think that the bigger the fountain, the bigger the wish it grants. What I love about my hometown's mall is that it isn't huge, but it still has enough stores to meet most needs, including an arcade and a second-floor roller-skating rink that hosted some of my birthday parties as a kid.

Record City, the music store where my friends and I take turns working shifts after school and on the weekends, is located between a candy store and Alton Books, a bookstore where I often go to browse during breaks. I've been an avid reader for most of my life. However, I dare not share with the guys my impressive *Goosebumps* collection piled high in my bedroom closet. They wouldn't get it since they would rather watch movies instead.

When I arrive, Record City feels like a ghost town. Dax, Monty, and Jordan are gathered around the counter, while Darryl, the manager, is unpacking boxes of new music in the back. CDs and cassettes are piled high, waiting to be sorted. He's in his second year of community college and hasn't quite figured out his plans after graduation. He seems like someone whose dreams don't extend beyond the city's edge — maybe even the mall's.

"Dax, would you stop goofing around and help me put away this inventory?" Darryl yells from the back of the store. "And don't get them all mixed up like last time. Madonna doesn't belong in the R&B section, no matter how hard she tries," Darryl huffs, pushing up his Coke bottle glasses, which are sliding down his face. Apparently, he broke his good pair and refuses to buy something more stylish. The same goes for his clothing. He typically wears the same thing every day: a flannel shirt over a band T-shirt and a pair of baggy jeans. He doesn't care much for fashion trends as he does for music. He could tell you when a song first aired on the radio, but couldn't tell you who Calvin Klein was. I admired that about him.

"Hey, guys," I said as I entered the store. I'm uncomfortably aware that the notebook in my backpack is still empty, which Monty wastes no time asking about. It annoys me how he acts like songwriting is such an easy task. I'd like to see him try.

Monty is twirling around on the stool behind the counter. His hair hangs over his face, which he swats away whenever it falls in front of his eyes. I watch as it swirls around in the air like a mop in a bucket. Like me, he wears similar clothing and brands. The only difference is that his clothes are usually covered in rips and stains from skateboarding falls. He isn't vain and doesn't care about his appearance. He believes the rips and stains are just memories, reminding him of his flips and falls.

"Where the hell were you today?" Dax pipes up as soon as he sees me. "I thought you were trying to bail on us."

Dax is the friend in the group who surprises me the most. Before befriending Monty and Jordan, we both played on the baseball team. He was the captain, and I played first base. He had an impressive record and probably would've earned a scholarship if he had stayed committed, which is why I was surprised when he left the team for good. Not to mention, girls were always into him, comparing him to Jason Priestley as if he had just stepped off the set of *90210*. I didn't have much trouble in that department either, but he liked the attention more than I did.

"I was exhausted. Fell back asleep." I shrug, running my fingers through my hair like a comb.

"So, let's see what you've got." Monty holds out his hand before Dax swipes it away. I think he could tell from the look in my eyes that I had nothing to show them. Dax and I know each other better than we'd like to admit.

"We need to start rehearsing something, otherwise, what's the point?" Jordan chimes in. "What if we had gigs lined up?"

"You're not serious?" Monty rolls his eyes. "We're not ready for all of that."

"Exactly." Dax nudges Jordan in the shoulder. "We don't even have a name for the band yet."

"Then why don't we focus on that before I start writing a bunch of songs?" I say, hoping that changing the subject will keep me from having to explain my writer's block dilemma.

"You're right," Dax agrees, "So, what do you guys think? What should we call ourselves?"

For the next hour, between helping customers and dodging scowls from Darryl, we tossed around a bunch of name ideas that, unfortunately, didn't stick. We even went so far as to browse all the CDs in the store for inspiration. We went from Aqua to the Wu-Tang Clan with barely a spark of an idea.

"What if we use some skateboard moves?" Monty offers.

"Yeah, but what?" Dax asked. "It would need to be catchy."

Until now, skating was our thing. We lived and breathed everything related to skating. It was what we were known for. Now, the band has taken over while our decks gather dust. It wasn't that we fell out of love with it, but what kind of future did it really have? We weren't Tony Hawk good, yet the band seemed to fit that same pipe dream category.

"Do you think you will have at least one song by the weekend?" Monty looks at me, almost pleading. "Maybe it would inspire us to come up with a name?"

"Slight chance," I laugh, just as a few kids walk into the store. They head to the new release section, where they start listening to the singles through wired headphones hanging on the wall.

"Wait," — Dax jumps off the counter — "What did you just say?"

"What?" I asked him, confused. "About me writing a song?"

"Yeah." He steps closer to me. "Say it again."

"There's a slight chance?" I repeat with less conviction.

"Slight Chance," he repeated. "It's clever. It's catchy. It's ironic."

"Calm down, Alanis Morissette," Darryl yells from the back of the store. "Now get back to work!"

Chapter Eight
Now

There are no clocks in the studio because, to me, they stifle creativity. The studio is my escape where time isn't real — it's just a concept, an idea. I want to be free from time and space, as if I were on another planet altogether. But when I need to be somewhere, like today, that's not such a good idea.

Just like in "Field of Dreams," "If you build it, they will come—or he," whatever the line is (I was never a movie buff). But quiz me on "Dumb and Dumber", and I will recite the entire movie to you. Still, I always thought that if I built a studio in my basement, maybe the guys would come, but only Monty has. Why is that?

Playing with him without reuniting with the rest of the band feels empty. It's not the same. For years, he had been begging us to get our shit together. *Go to couples therapy*, he'd joke. Monty was the one who took the band's breakup harder than the rest of us. For years, he fell into pretty hard times, clinging to anything that remotely gave him the same euphoria as music did. Unfortunately, there wasn't anything like it. Once you have had a taste of music and fame, it's hard to find a substitute.

"Shit." Robbie glances at his watch. "It's almost dinner time."

"What time is dinner?" I ask.

"Now," he says, pointing at his watch as if his mom would be calling from upstairs to say it was ready.

"Well, there went the day." Monty smiled as he set down his drumsticks while I pulled the guitar strap over my head.

The music that filled the room over the past few hours was exhilarating. At first, Robbie was unsure of himself. He held back from feeling anything, but I told him that if he wanted to create something worth listening to, he had to feel something. But like me, he seems very closed off—like a locked door that has lost its key. Either way, he needed to be vulnerable and open up, while also willing to face his wounds. So, he took turns on the drums with Monty as if his drumsticks were scalpels, pouring his soul out. A few hours later, he set the sticks aside and joined me on the guitar. The microphones near our lips teased ideas of songs to be sung, but all we did was feel the music through melodies that blended into one another.

I hardly knew this kid, yet I felt oddly comforted by his presence. Music has that effect on people. It can sometimes bring people together better than words ever could. I watched his eyes light up when we played, just like a kid on Christmas morning when they see all the presents under the tree.

With newfound confidence, he sang our songs as if they were his own. That's when I realized we had created something truly special. I felt my words come to life again as they escaped from his lungs. The notes he hit reminded me of my "once upon a time" era. It felt like I was transported back in time, like I was seventeen years old again. It was as if no time had passed. It made me miss the guys. And it made me miss her even more.

"We wasted the whole day," Robbie said, hopping off his stool.

"We did no such thing. It was fun playing for a little while. I'm glad we did it." I patted him on the back.

"Oh yeah?" Monty looks over at me. "How do you feel?"

"I feel fine. Why?" I asked.

"Anything coming back to you now?" His eyes peer at me as if searching for something I wasn't quite sure I even had.

"Um, no, Céline Dion. What the hell are you even talking about?" I shake my head.

"Never mind." He waves me off, dismissing the conversation.

"I don't know about you, but I don't think I want to get on the road this late. You might have better luck trying to catch another bus," I say to Robbie. "I can bring you."

"Are you not going to leave anymore?" He furrows his brow.

"Yeah, I will probably just head out in the morning."

"Then, I'll do the same. You don't mind, do you?" His eyes widened as if I was about to hand him a ticket to the chocolate factory.

"And if you both don't mind, I think I'll join you. I have nothing better going on," Monty interjects.

I tilt my head at him because I already told him I didn't need him tagging along. But before I could say anything, Robbie exclaims, "Road trip!"

I took a deep breath and exhaled, knowing I was outnumbered. "Fine, Robbie, you can take a guest room, but I need you to call your parents and get their permission. It's not like they know me."

"It will be fine, trust me." He winks. "You're THE Luke Grant."

We walk back upstairs, and almost immediately, Robbie notices a closed door he hadn't seen before. "What's in there?" he turns to me and asks.

"Ugh," Monty sidesteps, moving between Robbie and the door. "It's nothing," he says, glancing from Robbie to me. His expression is stern, but it's not the kid's fault for being curious.

"So, *that's* where you plan to murder me?" Robbie laughs. "But really, what's in there?"

"It's fine," I tell Monty. "You can show him."

"Are you sure?" Monty's eyes widen like the doorway is about to be. I linger back as he leads Robbie inside the home library that I had custom-built when I bought the house.

"It's a library." Robbie turns to face me. "You made it seem like it was something dangerous."

"Well, he built it for *her*," Monty replies. "And memories can be dangerous."

"Her who?" Robbie peers at me.

"Anyone want pizza?" I ask as I head back to the kitchen, avoiding the question entirely.

The morning sun wakes me up faster than the alarm I set on my phone. I stay lying in bed, staring up at the ceiling. After a few minutes, I take a quick shower before heading downstairs to make coffee. The kitchen is still somewhat dark, but luckily, the blue light from the coffee pot shines like a beacon guiding my way.

My body leans against the island as I slowly take a few sips from my steaming, hot mug. Between sips, I start to doubt my journey again. I turn to look out the French doors leading to the back patio and remember how badly I wanted to grow a garden in my first house. Every morning, I went outside and tended to it, but nothing ever grew (unless you counted the weeds). Still, I faithfully cared for it as if I were expecting a bountiful harvest. Then, one day, I called *her* over when I noticed something growing.

Right in the middle of my garden, a small green stem sprouted from the dirt. Something finally grew after all the time I had spent working on it. I had to remember that things take time, both spiritually and musically, and I needed to give myself some grace during the process.

In this memory, she is with me, hugging me as if my biggest achievement in life was that tiny green stem. But when I look down, I realize it wasn't. Not even my music. Not even her.

But I rub my eyes as if they could erase a memory I keep convincing myself is just a lie. *It's a lie, right? There was no way she was...*

As I take another sip of my coffee, I realize it's important to remember, as I gaze at my reflection in the window, that things weren't always like this. I was in love once. It wasn't easy, to say the least. It carried the risk of destruction. The fear of cutting the wrong wire and everything exploding. For a long time, I had to hold back. There was a period when I couldn't be honest with her or anyone else, for that matter. After all, the heart wants what the heart wants. And damn, did I want her.

Timing has never been my strong suit. Something always pulls me in the opposite direction, and most often, that thing is fear. Now, there's a barrier—a wall I can't break through. I know it's there (I guess that's the first step), but how do I knock it down? (That's the next step I can't quite figure out.) Either way, I am desperate for answers. I want to free my heart from the feelings that have pounded against its tender flesh, causing a constant ache that I knew would eventually lead to an irreparable break.

Years ago, something happened. However, a lousy reporter spreading fake news painted a picture of me that made me look like a cheater. The subject became so sensitive that we treated it like lava—afraid to touch it and get burned.

I don't blame her for how she felt. It caused a constant fear that followed her like a shadow, tormenting her with worst-case scenarios. Some relationships are built to withstand storms and rough waters better, whether they're a large ship or a simple rowboat. Over time, I've learned that it's never about the size of the boat — it's what it's made of. We weren't an ocean liner, but I still would have sailed through troubled waters with her, even if all we were was a raft.

Then, an even bigger story hit the front page. I was portrayed as a villain. The media flocked to the story like hummingbirds to nectar. They wouldn't let it go. Stories emerged from every angle, making it hard to escape. Slight Chance was no longer just known for music. We became famous for various scandals, with only a slight chance of recovery.

No matter how hard I tried to reassure her, it still tore us apart. Living in the limelight means everything you do is under constant public scrutiny. Words, pictures, videos, and other media can be taken out of context to support any narrative a journalist wants to push. The guys and I were always told this would happen, but like any naive rock star starting this new career, you think it will never happen to you or that it won't affect you like it has affected others. Unfortunately, by the time I realized the damage those narratives had caused, I was emotionally overwhelmed.

Even though I knew the truth, I still understood her perspective. When we finally faced each other, she dismissed me as if I meant nothing. I wasn't even given a chance to defend myself fully. She might have been in pain, but I was in pain too. I had a beating heart with feelings, but I pushed them all aside to comfort her. I never once regretted it. I would do it all over again. I would still do it now.

Honesty and trust were important, and they were two things she and I always agreed on. But instead of that bump in the road strengthening our relationship, it swallowed us up like a pothole, dividing us so much that our pieces no longer fit together. Our once seamless puzzle had become unrecognizable. It was as if we had taken pieces from different boxes, claiming we had enough to recreate what we once had. But pain jagged our edges, sharpened our corners, and made it too difficult to fit together smoothly without forcing it. When things fit naturally, there's never a need for glue.

The break broke me.

The guys all told me I needed to give her space—that things would eventually sort themselves out. So, I forced myself to be patient. But it was hard. Whenever I thought of something funny or had something to share, she was the first person I thought of, but the last person I could call.

Sadly, she didn't try to contact me, and my patience was wearing thin. I couldn't help but wonder what I was holding onto when, clearly, my outstretched hand was met with no one reaching back.

It was then that I decided to walk away. I shut everyone out and never looked back. Well, sort of... At least, that's what I remember. I don't recall much from that time. It flashes in and out like a flickering candle. That's part of the reason why there's this wall in my mind that I can't break through. The puzzle pieces of my life haven't been whole in quite some time. Even now, I'm trying to see the picture clearly. I want to understand it all, piece by piece. I know my journal holds the answers; I just need the courage to revisit the pages.

I was finishing my second cup of coffee when Robbie walked into the kitchen, showered, and was ready to go. "It was like that room was made for me." He stretched as he sat down at the island. "Did you make coffee?"

"Sure, kid. What would you like?" I reached for the carafe.

"Cream and sugar," he says as he gets up to grab a remaining slice of pizza from the fridge. "I love cold pizza in the morning, don't you?"

"It's the best," I smile.

"Sure is!" Monty says as he enters the room with his hand outstretched. "I'll take one."

"It would be so nice to live here," Robbie says as he takes a sip of coffee. "I hope to have all of this someday."

I take a sip of my coffee while trying to hold back a laugh. "You're only seeing what's on the surface. This is all materialistic. There's more to life, you know?"

"I mean, I left a perfectly good house on the beach in California to come live with my high school friend," Monty smirks.

"You can go back," I said, pointing toward the door.

"Just say when," Monty laughed.

"Why does Monty even live with you?" Robbie asks me as he wipes a few small droplets of coffee off his chin.

"Good question. Maybe you should ask him since he hasn't told me."

Chapter Nine
1997

Sometimes, I think about things too much. I'm an overthinker at best, yet I rarely manage to turn my thoughts into clear solutions. At night, it gets worse. Words that come to me at night are like dreams, which tend to fade by morning.

Time seems to fade as I begin to sense a faint promise from a song. The melody lifts me away as if I'm dust scattered on the floor. Maybe I was overthinking this whole songwriting thing. Maybe it was just about feeling something. Love, maybe? Nope. I don't know what that's about.

The truth is, I had never been in love before. *Like?* Yep. *Lust?* Hell yeah. But *love*? Love was as fleeting to me as a thought in the night. If I ever did find love, I guess I didn't grab it quickly enough. So, how could I possibly write about something I had never experienced before? Or maybe I should focus on writing about never having felt it? Now, there's an idea.

As much as I would love to lie in bed all day and debate all of this, I knew I couldn't skip school two days in a row. I pulled the covers up to my chin and bunched my pillow into a ball. The sun has become relentless, but I give myself a few extra moments, resisting the pull. I'm not ready to start this day yet.

My mom yells from downstairs that I need to get moving. Immediately, I jump out of bed, with covers and pillows flying across the floor as I pace the room, holding my notebook. The blankets get caught between my feet, swishing back and forth with every step I take toward the door until I finally manage to break free.

I rush down the stairs and yank the phone off the wall, the cord nearly choking me in the process. I dial Dax's number and feel relieved that he answers instead of his overbearing mother. Every time I get her on the line, it takes about ten minutes of talking before she hands the phone to Dax, always reminding me that she's expecting a call and doesn't have call waiting.

"Dude, tell me you're not skipping again," he yawns into the phone.

"No, I'll be there. It's just," I pause, twirling the phone cord around my finger. "It's just that I can't do this. I can't be under this much pressure," I sigh so loudly I'm sure my mother could hear me from the next room.

"Seriously? What the hell changed? What happened? Did Monty start bugging you again?" he fires out several questions without taking a breath. "You know none of us can write a damn sentence, let alone a song, Luke."

"It's too much pressure," I repeat. "I don't think I have what it takes."

We ended the call a few minutes later so I could finish getting ready for school. I throw on some clothes, fix my hair with a dollop of L.A. Looks hair gel, and tousle it until it looks somewhat presentable. For the most part, I look pretty good. Once I'm satisfied with what I see in the mirror, I brush my teeth and head out of the bathroom, where I find Wilson lying in the hallway, waiting for me to pet him.

"I gotta go, boy," I say, bending down to pat him on the head. He looks up at me as if he understands before falling back asleep. "See you after school, buddy."

I pull into the school parking lot in my blue 1984 Ford Pickup. It starts loud and runs loud, and I hate the looks I get when I drive because you can seriously hear me from a mile away. It's embarrassing. But I really can't afford any repairs on it right now. Then again, I can barely afford to fill the tank, which reminds me that I should probably ask for more hours at the store.

I spot Monty's hatchback parked at the back of the student lot next to Dax's car. I grab my JanSport and sling it over my shoulders as I head inside the building. After my call with Dax, I know he didn't waste any time telling the other guys. I'll have to face the music (or lack thereof).

As expected, the guys are lingering around my locker like feeder fish to a shark. I part the seas before entering my combination and releasing the lock with a satisfying click as the door swings open to reveal pictures of local and mainstream bands, concert ticket stubs, and a few guitar picks taped inside.

The hallways are lively with our classmates chatting and passing notes before the start of the day. School posters about activities, games, and upcoming events decorate the walls, but I never read them. Perpendicular to my locker group is my ex, Stephanie's. Usually, I try to avoid this area when she's around, but mornings are especially tough.

"All right, dude. What's the deal?" Monty leans against the neighboring locker. "Are you getting cold feet or something?"

"You guys need to find someone else to write the music. I can't do it," I say as I slide out a few textbooks.

"How about you let me decide since I will be the one singing whatever you write," Dax pipes up.

"Hard to sing a blank page." I roll my eyes.

"Well, you need to figure something out," Monty states as Dax immediately elbows him in the side. "*Ouch*. What the hell was that for?" He rubs his side.

"Luke just needs more time," Dax affirms. "Let's just ease off him, OK?" He places his hand on my shoulder as if trying to comfort me. "You will get there, man. I know you will."

"Slight chance," I reply, shutting my locker and heading toward homeroom.

Pun intended.

I arrived at homeroom to find the classroom already halfway full. A short kid with glasses sits in the middle row, who doesn't seem interested in making eye contact with anyone. He has bushy brown hair and is dressed like he's about to go on a job interview, while I'm wearing ripped jeans, a pair of Etnies, and a hoodie.

I decide to sit toward the back of the room just as the rest of the class starts to come in. And just like every morning for the past two months, Chase Matthews intentionally bumps into my desk, knocking over my books.

Chase Matthews is known for two things: being the captain of the lacrosse team and being a huge asshole. Not to mention, he's also the same guy my ex, Stephanie, cheated on me with. So, I guess, three things?

At first, I couldn't understand what she saw in him. Chase and I are complete opposites. He wears designer clothes, always making sure the Moose and Seagull logos are prominently displayed, like badges of pride.

Stephanie, however, was always middle of the road—meaning she could move between cliques and fit in wherever she landed. I always thought she fit in well with mine, but after everything that happened with Chase, it became clear she was more superficial than I initially believed.

After everyone settles into their seats and attendance is taken, the day drags on as it usually does. As much as I try to pay attention in class, all I can think about is my empty notebook. I remember my creative writing lessons and how each story needed a purpose; otherwise, what's the point of telling it? Maybe I should start there?

When school finally ends for the day, I head out to the parking lot when I hear my name being called. Without turning around, I already know whose voice it is. It's the same voice that occasionally echoes through my mind from time to time. I am almost tempted to ignore it and drive away.

"Luke!" the voice calls out again.

I turned around and nodded in her direction. It's Stephanie. "Hey," I say. I have no desire to talk to her. The image of me catching her cheating still pops into my head, but I refuse to let her know that I'm still upset with her about it, or even how Chase likes to torment me whenever he gets the chance.

"Hey," she says as she catches up with me.

As much as I hate to admit it, she looks incredible. Her skin is bronzed, and her hair is freshly highlighted. For a moment, I feel a bit envious of her jock-headed boyfriend, but I quickly remind myself why she and I are no longer together.

"I just got back from Florida with my family," she says, as if I asked or even cared to know. She fiddles with the hemp choker around her neck.

I tighten the strap of my backpack on my shoulder. I understand exactly why she approached me. It's almost like a pattern whenever she and Chase have a falling-out. It's as if she wants to see me hurt, because it somehow boosts her confidence to know she still has someone attracted to her. But I've learned not to show her any more emotion. I refuse to give her the satisfaction or the power to keep hurting me. I'm ready to move forward. I don't care anymore about her or what she does with Chase, for that matter. In my view, they deserve each other.

"I overheard Dax in the Science Lab talking about you guys starting a band?" she asks, looking up at me expectantly.

"Yeah. Why do you care?" I ask, doing my best to sound nonchalant.

"I just thought it was—"

But I cut her off. "Stephanie, I don't know why you're even talking to me. Go talk to Chase." I point back toward the school.

"Why are you being so mean to me?" she asks, stepping back with her hands on her hips. Her glittery eyeshadow catches the sunlight and shimmers across her lid.

"Let's see." I step closer to her. "You cheated on me. So, why would I be nice to you?"

She snaps a wad of gum in her mouth. "You're still angry about that? It was nothing, Luke. It was a dumb kiss. And besides, we were on a break."

"No," I correct her, "we had an argument. There was no mention of a break. So, keep telling yourself that, Ross."

"But I still love you," she says, pulling on my arm as I walk toward my truck.

"Seriously? Stephanie, you ended up dating him. And you still are!" I say as I release my arm from her grasp.

"Well, you broke up with me," she says as if it's all my fault.

"And for good reason," I huff.

"Luke, I still love you," she repeats as if I didn't hear her the first time.

I take another step toward her and close the small gap between us. "You don't know what love is," I say. But to be fair, neither do I. I just knew that love didn't involve cheating.

"How can you say that?" She frowns.

I really didn't want to deal with this right now. I pull my keys out of my pocket and open my truck door. I don't care that Stephanie is trying to tell me she loves me because I know she doesn't mean it. Come next week, she and Chase will get back together, and she will pretend like I don't exist again. I'm almost sure Chase wouldn't be happy to know that she comes running back to me whenever they are on the outs; he'd probably overturn my desk instead of just bumping into it.

I toss my bag into my truck and climb in. I start it up and hear the muffler roar to life, drowning out the sounds of the cars around me. I leave as quickly as I can. The only downside is that the faster I drive, the louder it gets.

Sometimes, goodbyes are louder than we intend.

Chapter Ten
Now

The three of us pile into my truck. Monty suggested we take his SUV, but I quickly nixed that idea. There's no way I'm not taking my truck. I'm already out of my element. No point in making it worse.

We roll down the windows, feeling the breeze through our hair and the freedom that comes from steering our own path. Monty sits in the backseat after Robbie claimed shotgun before we even stepped out of the house.

I have to admit, Robbie is an easy companion. He fits in seamlessly as if this is a common occurrence. He reminds me a lot of myself (or, at least, who I once was, that is). But even with all that I know now, the lessons he needs are not meant for him to grasp just yet. At least, they never did for me at that age. He needs to live a little longer. He needs to fail much more. He needs to learn lessons through all of that rather than being force-fed self-help examples. I could tell him everything that he needs to know, but it won't make a damn bit of difference. He isn't ready for all of that. His time will come, and when it does, he will know it.

So, for now, as much as I wish I could give him the playbook on life with a career in music, it's not exactly black and white. Hell, it isn't even gray. It's a kaleidoscope of colors that shift with every twist and turn.

Monty sits in the back like an old dog, peeking his head out the window and popping up between Robbie and me whenever he has something to say. He has always had a very energetic spirit that hasn't eased up at all. Married twice and divorced twice, Monty was always a free spirit who, when it came to color, saw the world in technicolor instead of black and white.

The radio is turned to a low volume, but none of us feels the need to turn it up. It functions like white noise—a gentle wave crashing against the shores of our minds. Robbie breaks the silence by starting to talk about his musical future.

"Well, statistically, you're more likely to get a job as an accountant than succeed in the music industry," I say. It was a tough truth, but he needed to hear it.

"That's exactly what my mom says to me. Although half the time I feel like she is holding out on me, like she wants to support me, but something always holds her back from giving me her full support. She told me once that she wanted to become a writer when she was my age, so maybe she is trying to prevent me from falling in love with a dream that can't be fulfilled?" he said, pressing his lips together in contemplation.

"Well, in your mom's defense, creative careers are more difficult. There are no job applications for becoming a famous author or musician. It's all about talent," Monty states.

"And luck," I interject. "Talent matters, yes. But even the most talented people don't get recognized. It's a tough business that doesn't make any sense."

"We just need a breakout song," Robbie grimaces as if he suddenly has it all figured out. "We need a hit. Then, everything will be fine."

"It takes more than one hit," I counter.

"What was your breakout song?" he asks.

"'Pivot.'" I smile.

"'Pivot?' Please tell me more." He ushers me on.

Well, I was a huge fan of Friends back in the day. The song was inspired by Ross and Rachel and their cult-famous 'break.' "Pivot" was just another scene from the series, so I took them both and wrote the song. It's a play on words." I shrug as if the concept wasn't a big deal, although at the time, it took me months to come up with. When I finally wrote it, the words poured out of me as if they had been waiting inside all along.

"So, I have to ask, why do you two live together? Aren't you too old for roommates?" he asks as if his words were like tiptoes across hot coals.

"It just works for us." Monty clears his throat. "For now, at least."

"And that library—what was that all about?" Robbie cocks his head toward me.

Honestly, I want to explain to him how I got here and emphasize the importance of the home library, but I struggle to find the words for my hardships. I can't help but wonder if talking about it might highlight my failures, making my life seem less remarkable than it actually was. And the last thing I want is for someone else to doubt this journey—everything I hold sacred.

I take a deep breath, staring straight at the road ahead. Once again, I feel Robbie's eyes welcoming me with their steady kindness. But I remind myself that he's just a kid. Still, something about him feels understanding and accepting, as if no matter what I say, he won't judge me. The words slip out before I can stop them. He watches me as if I've been put under a spotlight, which is something I've never felt off-stage (the spotlight tends to fade as soon as you step off).

Nevertheless, I found myself explaining everything he wanted to know, and maybe some things he didn't. And how this journey marks both the beginning and the end of some major parts of my life.

Monty leans back with his hands behind his head, fully aware that he and I have had this exact discussion more times than we care to admit. He understands this journey well. He knows all about the songs in my journal. In fact, I'm pretty sure he was the one who leaked it to the press. I'm not mad if he did. He knew I needed a push, and this was the only way he knew how to "push" me.

"You really know how to self-sabotage yourself," Robbie says to me.

"Excuse me?" I snap, almost slamming on the brakes. "I don't think you know what you're talking about," I respond.

"Now, wait a second," Monty interrupts. "Let's hear him out."

"For starters, you need to admit that *you* are the problem," Robbie says pointedly.

"Well, I like where this is going already," Monty laughs from the backseat.

"That's a little presumptuous, don't you think?" I ask.

"Let me explain." He turns to face me in his seat. "You've been in love with this girl for decades, and you wasted all that time because you were scared. Wouldn't it have been better to know if she felt the same?"

"Well, if I could say one thing—" Monty begins.

"You don't need to say anything," I cut him off.

"Two words," he says to me while peering through the rearview mirror. "Emotional debriefing."

"Either way, it's been too painful to figure out where she stands," I continue.

"More painful than spending your life alone? Because that's what you've been doing, right? Spending your life alone?" he asks as if he's trying to catch me in a lie.

"Some things are better discovered on our own," Monty says. His words drift around inside the truck, hoping they'll land on me.

"Like my lesson in music?" Robbie chuckles.

"Exactly," I agree. "Even if you believe music is your purpose in life, you still have to work hard for it. But that doesn't mean you should exhaust yourself in the process. You need to embrace both the good and bad moments and turn them into inspiration. Let it fuel your music."

"Is that what you did with your broken heart?" he asks.

"I think it's better if I tell you the story through my music." I reached into my backpack and pulled out my leather journal. "This is the story. This is everything."

"Shit," Robbie says, grabbing the journal. "This really is everything?"

"It's everything," I affirm.

"When was the last time you read it?" he asks.

I glance back at Monty through the rearview mirror. "It's been a while," I finally say.

"Which is why you probably should have done some light reading before hitting the road," Monty murmurs from the back.

"Oh, yeah? And what good would that have done?" I ask him.

"For one, you'd probably be— oh, wait, what were those two words again?" he mocks as I roll my eyes. "Oh, yes," he continues, "emotionally debriefed? Were they the words? But whatever, don't listen to me."

"Why don't you just tell me, huh?" I shot back. "If there's something I need to know, then why don't you just tell me? Why do you need to act all secretive?"

"It's not about being secretive. I was just told you should figure things out on your own. It's like testing the waters before jumping in. Telling you would be like pushing you right in—a shock to your system," he responds.

"Goosebumps?" Robbie interrupts as he opens my journal and flips to the first song. "What kind of song title is that?"

"You had to have been there, kid," I chuckle. "But seriously, Monty, what the hell are you talking about? And who told you that?"

Chapter Eleven
1997

The first few snowflakes of the winter season drift through the air, similar to the leaves that had just fallen not long ago. However, none of the snow sticks. Their presence is merely a warning that winter is approaching, and autumn will soon be ending.

When I pull into my driveway, I notice the new neighbors are officially moving into the house next door. I watch as the movers carry boxes back and forth from the truck into the garage. However, one of the boxes being handed off seems to be on the verge of collapsing. Sure enough, it breaks under the weight of whatever it was holding, and a few items fall onto the driveway.

There was no way the movers didn't see this, nor did I wait long to find out. I walked over to pick up whatever had fallen, thinking it would be a friendly way to introduce myself to the new neighbors. They couldn't be any worse than their predecessors. Fingers crossed. But I can't stop laughing at what fell out. What had fallen were a couple of *Goosebumps* books—my favorite.

My knuckles kiss the surface of the wooden door, but they don't produce much of a sound. I tried again, but this time, it was much louder. However, just as I go to knock again, I can hear footsteps approaching the door. It swings open, and I'm suddenly face-to-face with the most beautiful girl I have ever seen. She is slightly shorter than I am, with reddish-brown hair and green eyes. Her hair is tied up in a messy bun on her head, and she is wearing a Nirvana t-shirt. My heart immediately melts. Fuck it, it evaporated. It can't decide whether to focus on her or the books I'm holding. Therefore, I avert my gaze as my cheeks burn red. The mere sight of her has rendered me momentarily speechless.

Like a complete idiot, I just stand there. I'm struggling to form a single sentence as my mouth remains slightly agape, as though I've been frozen in place. I'm in shock. The blood that previously rushed to my cheeks swiftly disappears, and I'm afraid of where it's planning to go.

"I'm sorry to bother you." I clear my throat while trying to wipe the sweat off my hands onto my jeans. "I was pulling into my driveway when I noticed these had fallen from your moving truck." I quickly hand over the books before they get soaked in my grasp.

She takes them. "You live next door?" she asks me.

Honestly, what the fuck is wrong with you, Luke? Say something! My lips and brain refuse to cooperate. All I do is stare awkwardly at her, which makes me seem even more of an idiot. But I have to say something. Otherwise, I wouldn't blame her if she decided to shut the door in my face.

I nodded as my voice finally cracked out a response. "Yeah, I do." I point toward my house.

"So, you go to Redburn High, then?" she leans against the doorframe.

I nodded again.

"Nice. I'm starting there on Monday. Junior?" she asks, looking at me for confirmation.

"Yep. You?" I clench my jaw tightly as I feel my teeth grind against each other nervously.

"I am," she says as she looks down at the books. "Well, thank you for bringing these over. I would have been pissed if something happened to them."

"They're yours?" I ask before she shuts the door in my face.

"What?" She tilts her head at me, as if I'm about to make fun of her. "Do you have a problem with R.L. Stine?"

I laugh, nearly tripping over myself in the process. "A problem? Yeah, more like an obsession." My words come out in a jumble of excitement. If there was ever a moment to believe in love at first sight, I am confident that this would be it.

She grins. "Great answer. I have a pretty decent collection."

"Same," I say. "By the way, what's your name?"

"Elena," she says.

"Elena," I repeat. Her name tastes as sweet as honey in my mouth. "I'm Luke."

"Well, Luke, my parents and I are going to order a pizza. Would you like to come in and help my dad move some things around before he forces me to?" she smiles. "My mom and I are only good at pointing," she laughs, and I melt even more.

"Absolutely."

The movers didn't do much to help Elena and her family get settled. They carried boxes and furniture into the house but never asked where they wanted anything to go. So, for the next two hours, I helped Elena's father, Mr. Madison, move furniture and boxes into their assigned rooms.

"You were such a big help, Luke." Elena's father pats me on the back after he sets the boxes of pizza that were just delivered onto the counter.

"It was no problem," I say. "Glad to help."

After serving the pizza, I find myself sitting on the floor, leaning against a box in the living room, browsing Elena's collection of books. We instantly connected over our likes and dislikes, as if it were our private book club.

The whole time, I couldn't help but notice a small dimple on her cheek whenever she talked, chewed, or even smiled. I love it. Having once been strangers, we began talking and laughing as if we had known each other for years. And for the first time in a while, I felt a real connection with someone. The laughter felt intimate. The words sounded seductive, as if they had the power to strip away my vulnerabilities (and even my clothes). The ease of our conversation was unlike any I had experienced before. With Stephanie, we always discussed her interests, while she bypassed mine as if they were just billboards on an open highway.

When it's time for me to leave, Elena walks me to the door while her parents are busy unpacking boxes upstairs.

"Thanks again for helping. You really didn't need to," she says. "I'm sure you had better things to do with your night."

"It's fine. Luckily for you, I had nothing better to do," I laugh, but it's obvious my joke didn't land well.

"I guess I will see you around?" she says as she opens the front door to lead me out.

For some strange reason, I reach for her hand as if it's a gesture I'm used to extending. Her skin feels soft and warm, and for a moment, I think I see her cherry-red lips curl into a smile, revealing her perfect white teeth. Her complexion is golden, highlighting the honey-colored streaks in her hair. Her eyes are unlike anything I've ever seen. Sometimes they seem green, other times gray. But right now, they shimmer with a copper hue reminiscent of a sunset. It's like a beautifully painted canvas I could lose myself in. She truly is a work of art.

I let go of her hand as the touch of her skin sears the memory into me. "You will," I say. "Definitely."

The week fades into the weekend, like a watermark on a page. Wilson whines at my bedroom door, eager to go outside. The sun barely peeks through my bedroom blinds, and even though I could sleep in, I still make myself get up.

When I go downstairs, I see my stepdad, Frank, sitting on the couch, drinking coffee. The news was muted while he watched, reading the crappy subtitles that pop up every few seconds.

"You're up early," Frank says as I head into the kitchen to pour myself a cup of coffee.

"Wilson wanted to go outside, and I couldn't go back to sleep anyway," I say before taking a sip. I sink into the couch beside him.

"Mom told me you were over at the new neighbor's helping them move in," he says, straightening his tie as he speaks.

"Don't worry. They are nothing like the Garrisons," I chuckle. "I don't think they will bother you about the lawn — not that anything was ever wrong with it."

"That's a relief," he smiles. "Although, don't think your mother and I didn't see that goofy look on your face when you were walking back home."

"I didn't have a goofy look." I roll my eyes.

"You did, kid." He pats me on the knee, "You sure did."

After Frank leaves for work, I bring my notebook into the kitchen and sit down in front of it. My fingers brush the cover, but I don't reach for my pen yet, worried I might scare it away. I remember what my creative writing teacher once told us about feeling being the best inspiration for writing. And after last night, I was feeling A LOT. Butterflies? Check. Nervous anxiety? Check, check. A disease of the heart yet to be diagnosed? Check, check, and check. Elena. Elena. ELENA.

I couldn't stop thinking about Elena from the moment I walked away from her house. I should have asked her out, but I was afraid it was too soon. She hadn't even unpacked yet. Still, I know her favorite ice cream is black raspberry; her favorite show is *TGIF* (which is a block of shows, but I let it slide). I also know she reads a book a week. These small insights into who she is barely scratch the surface of who she truly is. I wanted to learn more about her, but I also wanted to take my time. After all, she just moved in, so she wasn't going anywhere anytime soon.

Mom kisses me on the forehead as she heads to the coffee maker. "Good morning," she says. "Good time last night?" She sits down beside me. "Looks like you made quite an impression on our new neighbors," she smiles behind her coffee mug.

I rolled my eyes for the second time this morning. "Let me guess, I had a goofy look on my face?"

She raises her hands defensively. "You said it. Not me," she laughs. "So, do you work today?"

"No." I shake my head. "I was actually planning to go down to the lake to do some writing, though."

"The lake?" She looks at me, "Why the lake?"

"Well, it's supposed to be unseasonably warm today, and I thought a change of scenery might help with my writer's block." I shrug.

"Oh, yeah? And how is that going?" She takes another sip of her coffee.

"It's going."

"You must be feeling *something*." She winks.

Chapter Twelve
1997

The streetlight in front of my house illuminates the path from my driveway to the front door, where a small porch light is malfunctioning. It blinks in and out, as if desperate to become a strobe light. I can't remember the last time I did something this impulsive.

After tossing and turning all night, I decided to change my scenery, hoping it would help with my songwriting dilemma. So, I took advantage of the nice day and got out of the house (and my head). I fumbled with my truck key just as I heard my name being called.

"Hey." I wave as soon as I see Elena outside on her front porch with a book in her hand. "You're up early."

"Couldn't sleep. I'm not used to the new house yet," she says. "So, where are you headed so early?" She places her book on her lap.

"Heading to the lake to do some writing," I reply.

"Really?" Her head perks up. "Would you like some company?"

Elena and I find a nice shaded spot by the lake where she has her book, and I have my notebook. We don't talk much since we are absorbed in our activities. It isn't until the afternoon sun begins to fade that I realize how quickly time has flown by. A low growl rumbles in my stomach, reminding me that we missed lunch.

Looking down at my notebook, I realize I barely wrote anything the entire time we've been at the lake. In my defense, how could I? Elena's presence entranced me more than anything else. I doubt she sensed any of this or heard the sound of my heart trying to beat out of my chest whenever I look at her.

My attention briefly shifts to the surrounding park as a few joggers rush past the pier. When the small group passes, I look back at her, where she is sitting with her book under a large tree. She is sprawled out on a park bench as if it were the perfect resting spot. I keep my eyes locked on her as if she belonged to me.

Elena is truly perfect in every way. In less than a week, I constantly wonder if she is just a figment of my imagination. Just sitting near her now, I have to pinch myself. I wonder if anyone else has felt the same way about her as I do. I wouldn't doubt it. Like I said, she was perfect.

She is reading *Beware, the Snowman,* a Goosebumps book released earlier this year. As she reads, she twirls her hair around her finger until she's ready to turn to the next page. Her auburn hair glistens in the fading sunlight, and it looks as though tiny strands of diamonds are woven throughout it. *Again, is she real?* Either way, I let myself linger in this "mirage" while I try to make out the expression on her face. *Is she happy?* But since she is so engrossed in her book, it's hard for me to tell.

I've long since given up writing, and I'm only snapped out of my trance when she hastily gets up from the bench and starts walking toward the pier. She turns to me and smiles, but there's something in her smile that pulls me out of my seat as well. Before I realize it, I'm walking down the pier toward her, as if she's a siren luring me to my doom.

Without any other explanation than me possibly experiencing a sudden out-of-body experience, I softly placed my hand upon her lower back. It rests there until she reaches over and wraps her arms around my waist. We stand there in silence, staring out into the water. It's at this moment that I know that heaven is real.

"It's really beautiful," she says, gazing across the lake. "I've never lived near a lake this nice before."

"It's not bad," I smirk.

Everything about this moment is breathtaking, especially how she and the view make me feel. I look down at the water as a gentle breeze flows through me, and I feel it running through my hair like a thick comb.

There's so much I want to say right now, but fear holds me back. We haven't known each other for very long. So, honestly, the fact that we're even embracing like this could only mean one of two things: We clicked immediately, or I'm dreaming.

With my luck, I'm dreaming.

Eventually, we sit side by side with our feet dangling off the pier. It's then that I forget everything else. I forget about the blank pages of my notebook. I forget how nervous I am. Just having her sitting beside me makes it impossible to focus on anything else. I honestly wouldn't want it any other way.

I watch as she closes her eyes and leans back, facing straight up toward the sky. The smile on her face makes my entire body break out in goosebumps. I shiver, rubbing at them while pretending it's from the cold.

Our hands are close together, and I feel a sudden urge to brush mine against hers as if I am unaware of how close we are. I imagine our fingers intertwined. I envy anyone who has ever held her hand before. I'm ashamed of these thoughts, especially if she just sees me as a friend. Still, I let my mind drift into endless wonder.

Eventually, she breaks the silence to tell me about the book she's reading. She speaks so passionately, as if she wrote the words herself. She shares vivid details about her favorite parts, which I listen to intently as if she's critiquing the next Great American Novel. To me, there's nothing sexier than someone who loves to read. It was one of the first things that drew me to her and one of the things that keeps me tethered. Again, goosebumps.

"How did your writing go?" she asks.

"Not that great," I laugh. "I barely wrote anything."

"You say that with such sadness. Is there anything I can do to help?" she looks at me. "I know we hardly know each other…"

"It's fine." I shrug.

"What are you writing, anyway? An essay for school?" She sits up straighter and looks directly at me.

"No." I shake my head. However, an essay sounds easier right now. "I'm trying to write songs."

"Songs?" Her eyes cut through the small space between us. "Do you sing?"

"I can," I smile. "But it's for my band. I'm responsible for writing the music."

"That is so cool." She leans back again, looking up at the sky. "I can still try to help, you know? I love to write."

We are no longer alone at the edge of the pier when we see two young kids start running down toward the spot where we are sitting. I hear their mom yelling from a short distance, telling them to slow down, but they ignore her. As soon as the taller of the two taps the other on the back, saying, "You're it!" the smaller kid crashes to the ground and scrapes his knee on the wooden planks. Seeing the fall, their mother rushes toward them to check the kid's knee.

"I told you both to slow down," she says, reaching into her bag to find a bandage.

"I fell because he pushed me," the younger kid whines as he points to his older brother.

"I didn't push you; I tagged you!"

"Well, we need to head back to the car because I don't have any bandages with me." She shakes her head and leads them down the pier, out of sight.

"Well, before our peace and quiet is disrupted for good, please let me help you," Elena says, looking directly into my eyes.

"Are you sure you want to help me?" I ask.

"Yes, I'd love to. I just can't believe you're a songwriter," she smiles as she says this. "I never would have guessed."

"Well, I also play guitar, and I sing backup vocals," I say. "The title of songwriter is still up in the air, considering I haven't written anything. But honestly, you don't have to help me."

"I want to," she replies. "Besides, I have nothing better to do." She winks at me before pulling me up from my seat. "Are you ready?"

"More than you know."

"Songs are not like movies or television shows, where you can see everything for yourself. The song needs to describe it— evoke the feelings. Otherwise, the words won't connect," Elena says as she plops down on my bed. Again, I have to pinch myself because I can't believe she is in my room, let alone on my bed.

"That's where the music comes into play," I cut in as if following the bouncing ball.

"Yes, but you need to learn how to express how you feel. So, why don't you describe to me how you feel right now?" she says, sitting cross-legged on my bed.

"Um," I hesitate, rubbing the back of my neck.

"Oh, come on," she nudges me on the shoulder. "Tell me."

I look around my bedroom, trying to think of something to say, because how can I honestly share my true feelings? I also don't want to disappoint her by saying nothing at all. So, I have no idea what to do as I navigate this uncharted territory. The only thing I know for sure is that I will probably look back on this moment as a wasted opportunity. She's literally asking me how I feel, and I'm just standing there like a deer caught in headlights.

"I feel lost," I say, not entirely sure where those exact words came from, but they arrived and lingered, showing no sign of leaving anytime soon.

"Lost?" She frowns. "What do you mean you feel lost?"

I shrug as if my words lack context, but she sees right through me, asking me to elaborate. Unfortunately, I don't want to.

"How about this? Close your eyes and pretend I'm not here. I want you to explain why you feel lost. Make me believe you. Make me feel like I'm lost too, and your words are about to find me," she instructs.

I take a deep breath. *Fuck.*

I close my eyes, and instantly feel like I'm on fire. All I can see in the darkness is Elena. If anyone were to find someone, she would find me. For reasons unknown, though, my mind shifts course, and I start rambling to fill the silence with any words I can find. I even go so far as mentioning my ex-girlfriend,

Stephanie, and how that relationship turned out to be a complete joke. It all pours out of me as easily as air escaping from my lungs.

"For a while, I thought I was to blame, but I knew with time that what she did had nothing to do with me," I say.

"No, what she did had nothing to do with you," she replies. "Have you dated anyone since?"

"No. Not that I'm against dating anyone new," I say while opening one eye to look at Elena. I wouldn't mind dating her, or kissing her, or holding her hand while telling her how hard I've fallen for her in such a short period of time. But I don't. I mean, that would be crazy, right? We've just met.

Instead, I slowly opened my eyes and see her staring at me. Her magnetic eyes hold mine and refuse to let go. I feel slightly embarrassed by everything I've said, and of course, by everything I didn't say. But I think it's too late. Elena catches on, and the way she places her hand on my shoulder, I can feel the compassion in her touch.

"Do you think people are honest about how they feel?" she asks.

I sit there, looking out my bedroom window. "It depends."

Without hesitation, she climbs off my bed and carefully heads toward my bedroom door.

"You're leaving?" I ask, upset by her sudden departure. I couldn't help but wonder if I had said something wrong or given her the wrong answer to her question.

She turns around and leans against my doorframe. "You don't give yourself enough credit," she says. "All you have to do is try."

"Try what?" I stand up from my spot on the bed.

"To be honest with how you feel," she says before turning around and shutting my bedroom door behind her.

My clothes cling to my skin as if they were glued there. I tug on the fabric as far as I can and try to wave in some cool air, but I know I can't handle the heat any longer. I'm nervous and sweating. When Elena left, I stayed sitting on my bed, scribbling a few words, but nothing worth keeping. I even doodled a bit before I closed my eyes and allowed myself to feel something other than tearing another page from my notebook.

For the rest of the night, I lose myself in the calming sounds of Matchbox 20, drifting through my thoughts, which spin around my mind like a CD in one endless and confusing loop. *It's 3 am, and I definitely feel lonely*. I eventually lean back and rest my head on my pillow. The soft, cottony sheets comfort me and ease some of the lingering ache in my mind. I can faintly smell her scent within the fibers.

The last girl I had in my room was Stephanie. We were on my bed listening to her new Spice Girls album. I laughed when she pointed out a few songs that she felt reminded her of me. Now, I wonder what it would have been like to do that very thing with Elena (certainly not listening to Spice Girls, that's for sure).

I may only have a twin bed, but there's now a strange emptiness, as if the possibility of sharing space no longer exists—like it was taken from me. I can't remember the last time

I cuddled or held hands with someone I truly cared about. I guess I'll never know what it would have been like if I had found the courage to try those things with Elena. For a moment, I let myself imagine Elena lying beside me. My arms are wrapped around her, and for the second time, I know what heaven feels like.

That's when I grabbed my pen, and the words started flowing.

> *Some might say I was without direction.*
> *No course found, no objection.*
> *Final destinations didn't matter to me.*
>
> *Some might say that I have wanderlust.*
> *No roots to plant, no time to trust.*
> *The fork in the road is nothing but imaginary.*
>
> *But with you, I have never felt more seen.*
> *And ever since you, my life has felt like a dream.*
> *I can't move. I'm frozen in place.*
> *Bags are unpacked. I'm home at last.*
>
> *Some might say I was lost, never to be found.*
> *No course to track; I'm homeward bound.*
> *Why go anywhere when you are right here with me?*
>
> *Some might say that I am bitter.*
> *The coldest heart. The harshest winter.*
> *But I never found anyone to warm me.*

Some might say that I am closed off.
Heart not open, tough to love
But I just never found anyone so worthy.

But with you, I have never felt more seen.
And since you, my life has felt like a dream.
I can't move. I'm frozen in place.
Bags are unpacked. I'm home at last.
There's no way any of this could be real.
My heart is shocked by what it could feel.

Like a mirage—an image I can't trust.
If I touch you, will you shatter into dust?
I shiver just thinking about how much you make me feel...
You are what I feel.
Goosebumps.

I set my pen down. My mind feels unexpectedly peaceful. I have nothing more to write, and that's okay. I don't even try to block the remaining thoughts that pop into my mind like CDs in a Discman. I don't obsess over what I wrote or what Elena meant when she told me to try. I feel strangely at ease, as if all the pieces of the puzzle are finally falling into place.

The song wasn't revolutionary (or was it?), but I felt it marked the start of something special. It was a perfect tribute to her.

A song she'd probably never get to hear.

Chapter Thirteen
1997

The school week flies by before I realize it, and I'm already back home. Wilson greets me at the door as I kick off my shoes and toss my bookbag nearby. Dax follows closely behind with a case of Surge and a new drink called Orbitz.

"I don't know, man. I've never drank anything with crap floating around in it. It seriously looks like backwash," I laugh, pushing away the bottle.

"Don't knock it until you try it." He shushes me before taking a big gulp. My top lip curls up in disgust.

A few minutes later, Jordan and Monty arrive. I know they are all hoping to jump right into the band stuff because the last few times we tried, we never got anything done (other than coming up with the band's name).

"So, what have you written?" Jordan asks with a mouthful of chips. "Or should we just trash this whole band idea?"

"You know, it's not that easy to come up with songs, ya know." My face reddens.

"Yeah, but you've already had a month," he says. "At this rate, we'll never get to play."

I place my Pepsi can on my lap as the outside condensation soaks into my jeans. My nostrils slightly flare, and my teeth gently clench. I lean back slowly to avoid spilling my soda, my lips twisting with annoyance as I glare in Jordan's direction.

He, however, is oblivious to my reaction as he starts reenacting a skit from last night's episode of *Who's Line is it Anyway?* I don't bother trying to explain myself, since he isn't really paying attention anyway. He's always had a short attention span—easily distracted by something else. But just as I am about to change the subject and tell them about my new neighbor, Elena, the doorbell rings. Wilson barks as I get up from the floor to answer it.

To my surprise, it's her, it's as if my thoughts somehow summoned her.

"Ugh, hi," she says as if she wasn't expecting me to answer. We hadn't really talked since that day she walked out of my room, nor had we really crossed paths at school.

"Hi," I respond, trying hard to hide my happiness at seeing her again. Seeing her again feels like fate brought her back to me.

Her gaze shifts behind me as if she's looking for someone specific. "Are your parents at home?"

"No. They went to dinner or something. Why? What's up?" I ask.

She shuffles her feet before asking. "You don't happen to have a plunger, do you? I can't find ours."

I can't help but laugh again as she nudges my shoulder.

"It's not what you think. I accidentally dropped my makeup brush in the toilet, and when I tried to fish it out, I accidentally flushed it." Her face turns crimson. "Do you have one or not?"

But I can't answer; I just laugh even harder. She hits me on the shoulder again.

"Ouch!" I chuckle. "Calm down, killer. So, you clogged the toilet, huh?" I wink at her.

She rolls her eyes. "I should have known better than to come over here."

"I'm just joking with you. But yeah, we have a plunger. Hold on." I leave her standing in the doorway as I go to find the plunger.

A few minutes later, Monty pokes his head into the bathroom. "What are you doing, Luke? Who's that hot girl at the door?"

"It's the neighbor. I'm looking for a plunger," I say just as I grab it from the bathroom closet.

"Why the hell does she need a plunger?" He leans his body against the doorframe.

"She needs to unclog the toilet," I say.

"Gross," he chuckles.

"It's not like that." I peer at him in her defense. No one is allowed to make fun of her but me.

Monty keeps asking me a hundred questions as we head back to the door where Dax is standing, talking with Elena. He runs his fingers through his hair (his signature move) while he laughs at whatever she's saying. Part of me wonders if I should be nervous about their interaction, but I quickly dismiss it. Elena and Dax wouldn't have anything in common, so I'm not worried.

"Here you go." I go to hand her the plunger, interrupting whatever conversation she is having with Dax.

"I'll take that," Dax intercepts the plunger. "All right, lead the way, my lady," he says as he heads out the door.

Elena pauses for a few seconds as I watch her open and close her mouth several times, as if she wants to say more. I try hard not to look at her rose-colored lips while wondering what they would feel like against mine. My mind starts to race. My palms begin to sweat. Maybe I am nervous?

"Do you need something else?" I ask, not realizing how harsh my question might sound, because almost immediately, her shoulders slumped as if I had said something wrong.

"Ugh, no," she finally says. "Thanks again for the plunger." She turns around and walks toward Dax, who's waiting for her in the driveway.

"What the hell just happened?" I asked, turning back toward the guys sprawled out on my living room couch.

"You know, Dax," Jordan says, looking at me. "He's probably going to ask her out."

"He wouldn't do that." I frown. "Would he?"

"She's hot. I would," Jordan replies.

"What, do you like her or something?" Monty reaches for a bag of chips.

"I hardly know her, but I wish I had been given the chance." I nervously start tapping my fingers on my lap, wondering what she and Dax might be talking about. "She literally just moved in..."

"Dax waits for no one. He's probably already asked her to marry him," Monty chuckles.

"That's not very helpful." I roll my eyes.

I feel extremely nervous—more than usual. I've never felt this way before. I barely know this girl, yet I worry that Dax might swoop in and take my chance with her (if there even is one). Then again, I have no claim over her. But something about her draws me in like a moth to a flame—not because she likes R.L. Stine or wears Nirvana T-shirts, but because there's more to her that I haven't uncovered yet. I want the chance to find out. Now, with Dax around, he might beat me to it because I've been too afraid to show how I really feel. Fuck it. I have to try. She told me to try!

Dax returns about twenty minutes later, soaked to the bone. I stop him at the door as he drips water all over the welcome mat.

"You are not coming any further covered in toilet water," I say as I join him on the porch.

"What? You think you could do any better?" he says, looking at me and shaking off the water still dripping from his arms.

"Well, I definitely wouldn't swim in the toilet," I joke, "But seriously, dude, what the hell did you do?"

"I was trying to fix it," he responds. "I guess I didn't know what I was doing."

"Wait, you didn't fix it?" I ask, realizing this could be my chance to jump in and save the day.

I push him aside and leave him on the porch as I hurry to Elena's. I reach for her door handle, where my hand trembles.

The cold metal presses against my fingers with an icy grip, but I don't pull away. I worry that if I retract my hand, I might lose the nerve to open the door completely. My fingers grasp the handle and turn. The turn is so slow that I hear the click of the metal joints moving inside the lock. The door opens slightly, then wider, until it's just large enough for me to step through. But my body stays on the porch. My legs feel stiff and heavy. I call out her name from the doorway.

"Elena?" I called her name again.

She peeks her head over the upstairs railing. "My parents are going to kill me!" she cries out. I don't know if she's actually crying or if it's toilet water on her face, but either one wouldn't be good.

"I came to help," I say as I take my shoes off by the door.

"Thank you," she beams. "I think your friend made an even bigger mess."

"He tends to do that," I joke.

I take a deep breath and walk up the stairs. Part of me worries I might embarrass myself, and if I do, I might as well tell my parents it's time to move. "OK, show me to the toilet."

She laughs at this, which I believe helped reduce the anxiety for both of us.

"So, you dropped a makeup brush down the toilet, huh?" I laugh some more as I reach for the plunger.

"I know. It sounds unbelievable, but it's true," she responds, somewhat confused. "My parents will be home soon, and they won't like it if they have to call a plumber. I hear they're expensive."

I am eager to say something helpful, but no words come to me. Surprise, surprise. "So, how are you liking school?" I say as I start working.

She shrugs. "It's fine." Silence settles around us, broken only by the suction noise from the plunger. I almost start to sweat. "I have met a few nice people, but not very many."

"You know me." I look up.

"I do." She smiles.

"I never knew you liked Nirvana by the way." I quickly change the subject as I try to get the water down again.

"Love them," she replies. "I feel bad for bothering you. I didn't realize you had friends over. I should have noticed all the cars parked in front of your house."

"Bother me? You could never bother me by the way," I say.

"Are you sure? You seemed upset earlier."

"Oh, that was about something else," I reply just as the toilet makes a loud gurgle, and the water begins to drain.

"Did you fix it?" Her eyes widened.

"I think so?" I flush the toilet, which seems to be working again.

"Luke! You're the best!" she shrieks as she throws herself into me. Her embrace makes my whole body tense up. I take a deep breath and start to relax. I can't help but wonder if she notices how my body responds to her touch. I'm now thinking about our time at the lake and the feeling of my hand on the small of her back...

"Seriously, thank you so much, Luke," she keeps going, snapping me back to the present. "If you ever need anything, I owe you big time."

"It's no big deal." I shrug and walk over to the sink to wash my hands. I realize that now could be my chance (if there is one) to ask her out. "Would you by any chance be interested in going to see a movie sometime or grabbing a bite to eat?" The words finally come out. I catch the scent of her perfume on me, and it's intoxicating.

She looks at me uncertainly, as if unsure how to reply.

My jaw tightens, and I feel my teeth grind nervously against each other. "Never mind. I'm sorry. I didn't mean to put you on the spot. You probably have better things to do," I say as if those words have become somewhat of an inside joke between us. But instead of replying, she moves closer. I can almost feel her breath on my skin, and against my better judgment, my heart flutters like a caged bird inside my chest.

"Wait," she says as she moves closer to me.

I'm unsure what to do. Is this the moment we're about to kiss? I quietly chuckle at the whole situation. My most romantic moment involves a clogged toilet. Her eyes sparkle at me as I find myself slowly falling into them until I hear her flush the toilet behind me, pulling me back to the present.

"Sorry. I had to double-check." She shrugs as if unaware of the moment I apparently shared without her.

"That's OK," I say. "So, what about that movie?"

"Oh, yeah." She steps back a few feet. "Well, I would, but your friend just asked me out."

"Dax?" I gasp.

"Yeah. I'm sorry. I just agreed to go out with him, and—" she stops abruptly. "I don't want to make things awkward, which I feel like they already are." She smiles at me, reaching for my hand. Still, I'm unsure what to make of her gesture. Her eyes catch the light above and almost twinkle at me. I pay more attention to that than her outstretched hand.

I can't remember the last time someone reached out their hand to me. Stephanie would always grab mine but never actually reach for it. In those moments, it always felt forced rather than something genuine. So, what do I think of Elena's gesture? The jury is still out on that one.

"It's OK. Really," I say, finally taking her hand loosely into my own. Her skin is so soft and warm, and I struggle to let go. I watch the way her lips curl into a broader smile, exposing the most perfect set of white teeth that I have ever laid my eyes on. Every time I look at her, I notice something even more beautiful than before. She is like one of those pictures that every time you move your eyes, you see something different.

"Are you sure? Because, well, I thought..." Her words feel as disconnected as my feelings. Her feet shuffle on the linoleum floor. Part of me feels like I know what she wants to say, and I would love to hear her say it, but I don't let the moment unfold that way. Still, it's nice to have someone hold my hand. It warms me. I guess I never realized how cold I really felt.

I slowly withdraw my hand and rest it by my side. The sensation of her skin leaves another memory etched in me (one I'm eager to forget). "I have to go," I say as I head out of the bathroom.

"What's the rush?" she asks as she follows me. I don't understand why she cares that I'm leaving, especially now that I know she's going out with Dax.

"Music calls." I look up at her once I'm back downstairs.

"Are you writing?" The interest flickers across her face.

"Yes. Thanks for helping me that day." My cheeks turn red. I'm annoyed with myself for missing my chance. "See you later," I say just as I grab my shoes and leave her house.

I closed the door behind me without saying another word, but it shut louder than I expected because of a sudden gust of wind. The wreath hanging on it knocks back into the door with a loud bang. I hesitate to open the door again and apologize, but I don't because I'm afraid I'll end up apologizing for much more.

I'm having trouble understanding what just happened. What exactly took place? The cold air presses against my face, almost freezing my frown in place. As I reach my front door, I stop. My legs feel almost rooted to the ground. Did Dax really ask the girl of my dreams out? He didn't even know how I felt, but shouldn't he have asked?

My breath quickens as racing thoughts flood my mind. My chest feels like a pile of books has fallen on it, and I struggle to catch my breath. I place my hand on my chest, feeling the heartbeat grow stronger. I quickly push open my front door and glance back toward her house. Should I have tried harder? Then again, there's a good chance it won't even work out. So, maybe none of this will matter in the long run. *Right?*

"You OK, dude?" Monty asks as he sees me by the door.

"Yeah. I'm fine," I lie. My emotions feel like they've been churned in an electric mixer. One moment, I was elated—excited about meeting someone as special as Elena. The next, I feel heartbroken. Is that even the right word for this feeling? But instead of being honest with Dax, I stay quiet.

For the next hour, I focus on my nemesis: the blank page. The whiteness is almost blinding as I stare at it, waiting for something to happen. It's as if I expect the words to appear on the lines before me instantaneously.

I rest my forehead on the page as if, through osmosis, the words from my mind would magically appear between the lines. I think about the first time I saw Elena. I remember the feeling of her breath lingering on my skin. I could almost feel the goosebumps reappearing all over my body. I'm not someone who falls easily. But with her, it was effortless, like I've been stuck in a weightless suspension.

Suddenly, the pressure begins to lift. I no longer feel the urge to toss my notebook aside and quit. Something feels different. It's a sensation that starts in my stomach and then shoots up to my chest before flowing down to my fingers. I move the pen across the page, and that's when the words start pouring out of me.

The clouds gather, darkening the sky as the snow draws near. Jordan peers out the window, fogging up the glass with his warm breath. "It's definitely going to snow," he says. "What should we do for the rest of the night?" He looks over at me, but I'm too lost in my thoughts to answer. My mind won't let my fingers rest, as if it's making up for lost time.

"I'm really sorry," I say, biting down on my pen.

"Sorry? What do you need to be sorry for?" Monty slaps me on the back. "You're writing! We might actually have a shot at starting to practice!"

"I think I need some time alone," I tell the guys. "I can't have you all hanging around me. It's distracting."

"Well, I have a date tomorrow, so I need to call and check the movie times." Dax winks at us. I doubt he knows how upset I feel, so I can't really be mad at him. "But are you sure, man? You look kind of pissed," Dax says to me. "Or is this how you normally look when you're writing?"

If I were smart, I would have taken this chance to tell him how I felt, but I didn't. And no matter how badly I want to drown out the thoughts telling me to do just that, my mouth betrays me, and through gritted teeth, I say, "Good luck on your date. Now, go," as I walk them all to the door and kick them out.

As night falls, darkness swarms my house like a cloud of insects. I quickly turn on some lights after spending the past few hours paralyzed on the couch. My chest still hurts. My heart pounds against it as if it's being held there against its will because I've been ignoring its wants and needs. The stress of the situation with Elena is taking a toll on me. I want to run. But where to exactly?

Eventually, I stepped into the shower, feeling the hot water burn into my skin. It pours down on me like a waterfall, mixing with the tears I didn't realize I was holding back. I think about my life. Everything about it has always been nothing but routine. There was no spontaneity and no surprises. And for years, I was okay with that. In fact, I thrived on it. But then Elena arrived and shook everything up. Now, I don't know how to find solid ground.

It's surprising that I already have such strong feelings for someone I hardly know. I can't believe I'm in this situation. I wasn't looking for love or even a relationship. In fact, I needed a break after Stephanie. I didn't see Elena coming, but she showed up anyway. Did I like her because she was new? Maybe I needed to figure out my feelings first before I made a mess of things.

Chapter Fourteen
Present

We pass billboard after billboard of pointless advertisements. I take a sip from my bottled water, but as I feel it trickle down my throat, something doesn't seem right. Did I forget something?

But that's impossible. I've packed for this trip more times than I can count, so I know I didn't forget anything. Then what could it possibly be?

I reach into my bag and pull out a few snacks, handing them around. I focus on the road, but I know my mind is somewhere else. I can't quite figure out where this feeling is coming from, but it keeps getting stronger. It's more of a distraction than seeing another billboard.

"I don't understand why you didn't tell your friend how you felt about her. I'm sure he would have backed off if you were honest," Robbie says to me as he takes a bite of his granola bar.

"Hindsight is 20/20, I'm afraid," I defend. "I just didn't know how to handle things back then."

"Yeah, but you really liked her. And from the sounds of it, she may have really liked you, too," he continues.

I shift in my seat. "What makes you think that?"

"Well, when you were telling us about the times you two were together, it was almost like she was hinting at her feelings, but you just didn't catch on. It sounds to me like you were too wrapped up in your own world, which made you overlook hers," he says with a mouthful of granola.

For the first time, I had never considered this before. The more I thought about it, the more it seemed plausible. Was I so caught up in my own feelings that I ignored hers? If that was the case, it's no wonder she agreed to go out with him initially. I was to blame. Me. And only me.

Monty, probably sensing my inner distress, switches the subject. It's funny how in tune he is with my emotions—more than I am myself.

Robbie pulls his laptop out of his bag and opens it. "I think this could make a great song. Don't you?"

"Or an album," Monty chuckles.

I always preferred notebooks when writing songs. Sure, I have a pretty decent laptop, but there's something more personal about a pen and a notebook. Every time I open a new notebook, I slowly drag my pen across the page as if it were the art of lyrical seduction. You really can't do that with a laptop.

Soon, we decided to stop at a rest area and stretch our legs. Robbie is hungry for lunch, so we choose to go inside and get something to eat. Often, I forget who I am and am surprised when I'm recognized out in public. Because as soon as Monty and I walk inside, people start flocking to us, asking for pictures and autographs. Too bad there isn't a rest stop for that.

"The way you describe her, it's like there's no other girl like her in the world." Robbie looks over at me with a mouthful of fries.

I set my drink down as my heart flutters, remembering the first time I ever laid eyes on her.

"You really loved that girl," Robbie says to me.

"*Love*," I correct him.

"And you have for so long," he frowns.

I lean back in my seat, my head drooping slightly as if weighed down by what I'm about to reveal. "I know," I finally say. "I've never stopped loving her. And there was a time," I gulp, "she loved me, too."

The pain radiating from everything I said leaves a tangible cloud around me like a cocoon. No matter how many times I tried to shoo it away, it stays as if it were made of lead.

"But can I ask one more thing before we head back on the road?" he asks.

I nodded. "Sure, kid."

"If you were so sure about how you felt, why did you doubt yourself so much?"

Chapter Fifteen
1997

I have an early shift at the mall today, so I wasn't surprised to see my stepdad on the couch watching the news at low volume again. It's becoming quite a routine for him. So, I grab a cup of coffee and join him, which is also becoming a routine of mine.

"Did you know they are predicting the end of the world again?" he laughs. "Apparently, when it becomes the year 2000, all the computers will reset and send us back to the Stone Age. Nuclear weapons will launch; banks will crash." He shakes his head. "It never ends."

"They didn't have computers in the Stone Age," I say.

"Good point." He takes a sip of his coffee. "You're up early."

"Yeah, I have a long shift today at Record City," I say.

"That will be a nice paycheck for you. By the way, how's the band coming along?" He turns the volume up slightly on the television.

"It's going. I finally finished some songs last night," I say.

"That's great. And what about your dilemma?" he asks.

"What dilemma?"

He smiles and nods toward Elena's house.

My nostrils flared as I bit my lip. "You know about that?"

"Well, you couldn't stop singing about it in your room last night." He nudges me on the side. "You sounded pretty good, by the way."

"Singing is Dax's job. And besides, I'm more comfortable being the backup," I said, taking another sip of my coffee.

"Are you?" he cocks his head at me. "Seems like you're taking that stance with a lot in your life right now."

There is something about the early hours at the mall that feels like you're entering an alternate universe. It is eerily quiet. You can actually hear the fountain water cascading into the pool below and cycling back again. There is no commotion. There are no shoppers meandering or rushing from one store to the next. Instead, the hour belongs to the employees and the early mall walkers, who tend to float around like the mall's unofficial ghosts.

Usually, an hour into the morning shift at Record City is when the foot traffic picks up unless it's an album release day, then it's chaos.

What I love about the store is its aesthetics. It isn't commercial, nor is it even a franchise. It's a single-location shop owned by a guy who simply loved music. The walls were painted a purplish hue that matched the carpeted tiles on the floor. Posters decorated the walls like artwork, and the smell was a mix of vinyl and the plastic packaging from the CDs and cassettes. It even had a small gadget aisle where I jumped on the Tamagotchi train and bought one of my own. Unfortunately, I never remembered to feed it, yet it still pooped every five minutes.

Darryl is already at the store when I arrive. Monty quickly follows, yawning as if he had sleepwalked there. He tosses his bag behind the counter and plops down into a chair.

Darryl assigns me the task of organizing the floor while Monty works at the counter—or seems to be sleeping there, based on the look of it. Halfway through my shift, I start to get distracted. I pay more attention to the people walking past the store; I compare the number of CDs to cassettes, and even keep track of how many M&Ms I've eaten all morning.

"You know you have to pay for those," Darryl says as he walks past me. He always says this, but never charges for what we eat in the store. Then again, judging by the number of wrappers I've accumulated, I think that's about to change.

When it's time for a break, Monty and I grab a couple of slices of pizza at the food court. I spin my drink with my straw as if every time the straw hits a piece of ice, I'm breaking down the barrier to my thoughts.

"What's going on with you, dude?" Monty asks with a mouthful of pizza. "Nervous about band practice tomorrow night?"

Shit. Band practice? I totally forgot. Just thinking about seeing Dax makes me nervous, especially since he and Elena planned to go to a movie tonight. I'd give anything to fall into a hole and vanish.

"I'm fine," I say as I hide behind my slice of pizza.

"You have songs we can start rehearsing, right?" Monty asks, as if that's the only thing I could possibly be worried about.

"I wrote about four." I swallow a huge bite of my pizza.

"That's great!" he exclaims. "So, what's your problem then?"

"I'm just tired." I fake a yawn, which he doesn't seem to question.

After he finishes eating, he sinks back into his chair as if he's examining me. "Actually, now that I think about it, you've been acting weird ever since last night when Dax came back from your—" he stops himself. "Wait…"

I try my best to avoid eye contact, but apparently, I'm being more obvious that way. However, if Monty could pick up on my behavioral shift, then why didn't Dax? I was the closest to him, after all.

"Oh, shit. You like her!" Monty claps his hands as if he's celebrating his discovery. "And now Dax is going out with her tonight." He runs his hand along his face.

"I know." I glance across the table at him. "But could you please keep it down?"

"No one knows who we are. Who cares?" He shrugs. "So, what are you going to do? Are you going to tell Dax?"

"And then what? Tell him he can't date my neighbor because I liked her first? This isn't like calling shotgun when you want the front seat," I huff.

"Isn't it, though?" he frowns.

"Trying to tell Dax how I feel would be pointless. There is no guarantee they will even start dating. I just need to wait it out," I say.

"Until when exactly? When the priest asks if anyone wants to speak now or forever hold their peace?" He shakes his head.

"Exactly." I chuckle.

"Solid plan, dude," he says, rolling his eyes. "I mean, no offense, but Dax knows how to lay the charm on thick. Even if you're not ready to tell her how you feel, you should at least tell Dax. Otherwise, you might lose your chance."

It takes a few seconds for what he said to sink in. "I don't know, Monty. There is no way she would go for him. They have nothing in common."

"You've heard the saying that opposites attract, right?"

Dax showed up at band practice the next day like he had just won the golden ticket to the Wonka Chocolate Factory. And when he smiled as wide as the Cheshire cat, I knew I was doomed.

I nervously sat down as he started sharing the details of his date. I folded my arms across my chest and then unfolded them, as if I couldn't decide what to do with them. I fidgeted enough that Monty noticed and softly tapped me on the back of my head, which only made me fidget more. However, my eyes didn't fixate on Dax. I couldn't look at him, fearing he'd see right through me. I didn't want to be that friend who falsely claims something about someone or something I have no right to. Even if I were honest, I'd feel so shallow. I can't imagine how those words of entitlement would taste if they came out of my mouth.

Nevertheless, my fear has come true. The date, according to Dax, went very well. They went to see *Titanic*, which must be the longest movie in history, since he mentioned they had an intermission. There was enough sadness to make her reach for his hand several times once the ships started sinking. It was a perfect setup for a successful date. By the time the movie ended, they were starving. So, they grabbed a bite to eat, all before he dropped her off and kissed her goodnight.

Dax fucking kissed Elena.

I want to die.

The best move I could make was to detach myself from the situation emotionally. I will concentrate on the music and nothing else. I will not look at Dax. He is just the band's lead singer. Nothing more. I will be a vessel to channel my emotions into songs that only Dax can bring to life (even if they are all about Elena). It doesn't make me a liar; it just makes me the bigger person.

Right?

"Let's see what you wrote." Dax holds out his hand for my notebook, but I don't move.

Monty has to practically nudge me on the shoulder to get me to snap back to reality. "Here," I say, reaching into my bag.

"So private," Dax teases. "You make it seem like I'm asking to read your diary."

If only he knew...

I fake a laugh as he holds my attention before opening my notebook to read the songs I had written. With each second that passes, my hands stay frozen at my sides. I try to peel them off, but it feels like I'm ripping my skin in the process. Unbeknownst to him, these are genuine feelings he's reading. I exhale deeply as he turns the page.

"Are you ready for what I think?" Dax looks up at me after he finishes reading. He closes the notebook and hands it back to me.

Monty and Jordan sit on the couch, anxiously waiting to hear what Dax has to say. However, Dax stands there smiling, as if he's waiting for me to give him permission to speak, as if I need to encourage him.

"You're a good writer, Luke," Dax says to me. "I mean, you know you're a good writer, right?" His confidence is tangible. I feel the certainty in his words and the assurances in his gestures, which somehow make me magically abandon all my previous reservations. I think about the songs I wrote and wonder if this is what stepping out of the darkness feels like.

I cling to his words as if someone could come in at any moment and take them away. Hearing my best friend say he believes in me makes me believe in myself even more. For the first time since we talked about starting a band, I truly feel we might have what it takes to succeed.

"But damn, dude," Dax grins, "I had no idea you liked Stephanie that much."

My eyes almost popped out of my skull. "Stephanie? Why would you think they're about her? They are actually about—" But instead of letting me finish, he cuts me off so we can start rehearsing.

In the days that pass, I don't say a word about my true feelings for Elena—even when I find out that she and Dax have been spending more time together. It's hard watching him drive her home from school or seeing his car parked in front of her house. It all feels invasive.

Often, she would come and listen to us play. I always enjoy seeing her, but not in these conditions. Sometimes, I would imagine she was there just watching me.

Dax asks me after reading my lyrics, "Is this song more like a ballad?"

"Not necessarily a ballad," I reply. "But you definitely need to sing it with some feeling."

He nods as if he understands. "Do you have a beat in mind?"

I grab my guitar and strum a few chords until I find the right notes. Once I have the intro somewhat figured out, I nod to Dax to jump in, but he can't find his voice. He hands me my notebook in defeat.

"You sing it. I need to hear how you imagine this sounding," he instructs.

I wasn't prepared for this—especially with Elena present. The last thing I want is to sing a song about my feelings for her in front of her. I have to be careful not to make eye contact. I will need to dissociate myself from the song as much as possible— and from her. Otherwise, everyone would know the truth.

I clear my throat. Saliva burns as it slides down my throat until it feels as dry as the Sahara. I focus on my notebook. I forget about trying to picture everyone in their underwear because if I even dare to imagine Elena in hers, I might catch fire. Instead, I picture myself completely alone in the room. There's no one here. I act as if I'm shouting my feelings into the emptiness.

You drew me in.
I don't know how or why, but you did.
You pulled me in and wouldn't let go.
You hold me captive
How or why, I do not know.

Just when I think you're about to release me
I'm tethered to you once again.
Because with you, there is always a beginning
With you, I hope there is never an end.

You drew me in
With your soft lips and effortless smile.
You've warmed the coldest parts of my soul

And have driven me wild.

I wonder what it would feel like
I wonder about the taste
I wonder if I were to pull you in
Would you let the moment go to waste?

I could hold you prisoner
Like you're keeping me shackled for life
I would do anything to make you happy
I promise to always treat you right

What a beautiful chance to open the door
To say that I love you, and that I want more.
I want to venture into every corner of your mind
I want to search the depths of your soul and leave nothing
behind.
I don't know how or why, but I do.

Just when I think you're about to release me
I come running back to you again
Because with you, I'll always be here
With you, my love will never end.

My lyrics feel vulgar and inappropriate. Was I confusing a confession with a song? Or vice versa? I wasn't sure. Either way, my words held beauty and depth. In a way, they felt poetic and just. Dax immediately signals to start again as he takes over the song like it's his own.

Hearing my words belt out from Dax's mouth makes me wonder if he would catch on to their meaning. I'm beginning to see that there are no longer any blurred lines between my feelings and the words I'm choosing to confess on paper. I need to navigate these waters carefully; otherwise, there's a real chance Dax would cut me from the band and his life.

I watch closely as she sits there, gazing at Dax in complete awe. She knows I wrote the song, but it's almost like she doesn't realize it. Love must cause some form of amnesia because she strangely acts as if the songs came from him.

Chapter Sixteen
1997

Stephanie called.

Twice.

She left a message on our answering machine, and honestly, I'm too emotionally drained to handle her drama.

But before I even reach my bedroom, there's a knock on the door. Two guesses who it might be.

Stephanie.

I opened the door to find her standing outside in her winter coat, hugging herself for extra warmth against the cold. Christmas is in two days, and I notice she is wearing holiday earrings that dangle from her ears. She smiles as soon as she sees me.

"I called," she says.

"I know." I watch her from the doorway as she starts to bounce slightly where she stands. I feel a few snowflakes land on my hand and melt. Looking up at the sky, I realize more snow is on the way.

"I don't know why I'm here," she laughs as she looks up at the sky and then toward me.

"Do you want to come in?" I ask because it's obvious she's freezing. The last thing I want is for her to freeze on my porch, and then I'm stuck with her forever. "Listen, Stephanie," I say as she steps inside. "I'm not trying to be an asshole, but what are you doing here?"

For a moment, she says nothing. I can feel her eyes on me as if she's searching for the right words, and I'm her map to find them.

"What is it, Stephanie?" Her facial expression shifts to something unrecognizable. Sadness? Guilt?

"Forget it. I shouldn't have come." She steps back toward the door. Snow melts off her shoes, leaving a puddle on the floor.

"You also called," I say, as if she shouldn't have done that either.

"I know. I rehearsed everything I wanted to say, but now I'm at a loss for words," she frowns.

"Just start somewhere," I coax.

She takes a deep breath. "OK, well, first I want to apologize to you for everything. I'm sorry for how I've treated you. You never deserved it."

"There is no need to apologize. It's all over and done with. *We* are over and done with," I add.

"So, you've moved on?" she asks, or maybe it's a statement lost in translation. I, however, say nothing because it's too complicated an answer to give.

"I never did," she admits. "After that night I kissed Chase, I knew you wouldn't want to be with me again. So, I stayed with him because I didn't want to be single."

Again, I say nothing.

"Well," she continues as if answering for me, "this is obviously bad timing on my part. She must be one lucky girl."

I really don't know how to process what's happening. I look at Stephanie, and for a brief moment, I remember why I liked her. She's pretty, smart, and can sometimes make me laugh without even trying. But then, just as quickly, I recall why I stopped liking her. She became self-absorbed. She grew too concerned with her popularity and what others thought of her more than anything else (or me). In return, I gradually became a filler for voids that were self-inflicted on her part. When I left baseball behind and took up skateboarding, I was quickly ostracized. Because of this, she made it seem like my decision was a risk to her social status. She barely acknowledged me at school, and the time we spent together decreased more and more. So, if I wasn't good enough for her then, I definitely wasn't going to be good enough now (not that her opinion reflected anything true about me). I just didn't want to share my energy with someone so superficial. It would be like breathing in parabens. I needed to pivot.

"I broke up with Chase," her words cut through the silence gradually building. "I don't know why I ever dated him."

"Well, you did," I say. "And you did for a while."

"I've just been wrong about everything. I was wrong about you, and I'm sorry." She runs her fingers under her eyes as a few small tears slip down her flushed cheeks. She tries to turn away before I can see, but it's too late.

Unfortunately, it's too late for many things.

Later that evening, I went outside to take out the trash. I see Elena's dad, Mr. Madison, hanging Christmas lights. "Better late than never," he calls over to me. "You wouldn't mind giving me a hand, would you, Luke?"

"Not at all," I say as I walk over to their front porch and help him string lights along the pillars and around the roofline. Christmas Eve is literally a day away, and the man wants to decorate. I have to give him props. I wouldn't see the point myself. My stepdad hung ours the day after Thanksgiving. He has always considered it a tradition.

After we finish, Elena greets us at the doorway with two mugs of hot chocolate. "Thanks, dear," Mr. Madison says to her. "Well, I'm going to take this inside. Thanks again for your help, Luke. It looks great!" He pats me on the back before heading inside.

"No problem," I say as I nervously take a sip.

Elena moves closer to me as a smile spreads across her face. Her eyes seem to stay fixed on mine as if they are too heavy to lift. I'm afraid to look back at her and risk what my expression might reveal. Still, I have no control over how much my heart races because of how beautiful she is.

"Are you mad at me?" she asks, her eyes sparkling under the Christmas lights. She could be the star at the top of the tree.

"No," I lie. "Why would I be mad?"

"I don't know." Her feet shuffle underneath her. "You seem different toward me. Is this about me and Dax?"

I hesitate at the question while taking another sip. The hot chocolate slides down my throat faster than I can swallow. It goes down roughly, making me cough uncontrollably. I feel a few droplets of hot chocolate trickle down my chin, which I quickly wipe away with the back of my hand.

"What makes you ask that?" I keep trying to clear my throat.

"Just a feeling," she shrugs. "If there's a problem or if there's something I should know…"

"Nope," I cut her off. "Dax is a great guy. You'd be foolish not to like him."

What the fuck is wrong with you, Luke?! She literally gave you an opening, and instead, you tell her she should like her best friend and not you! Are you an idiot?!

She nods her head as I take another sip to soothe the tickle in my throat. "Well, how is your writing going?" she changes the subject.

"It's going," I reply. "Thanks again for helping me that day."

"Do you still need my help?" she asks, looking at me expectantly, as a sudden look of eagerness takes over her face. "I really enjoyed it."

"No, I'm good," I say.

"You *are* mad at me," she states. "Because if you aren't, you're acting very differently toward me."

"Why do you want to help me, Elena? Do you need something from me in return?" I ask.

"Seriously?" she says, as she steps back from me.

"It's just that you haven't asked for anything in return, and I've noticed that most people do things for others when they expect something back," I explain.

"Whoever said that I wanted something in return?" she scoffs, placing her hand on her hip.

"That's right. What could you possibly need from me? I guess besides fixing your toilet?" I ask.

"Are you serious?" Her mouth hangs open.

"You know nothing about me, Elena. I am nothing but a stranger to you, yet—"

"Yet, what?"

"You're not to me. Yes, you've helped me, and I appreciate it more than I can say, but how can I—*Ugh*, how do I explain this? People in my life—people I've loved—" my voice breaks for a second—"have always made me feel like no good deed goes unpunished."

Elena leans against her porch railing. Her eyes don't immediately meet mine, but I can tell she's considering what she wants to say in response. I've already said too much, yet not enough at the same time. My head hangs slightly low, and I wish I could take it all back. Like a magician shoving all his scarves back into his hat, I wish I could push all the words back in. The pain radiating from everything I've said (and not said) builds an invisible wall between us, separating us even more.

Way to go. Luke.

"Why do you feel that for someone to do something nice for you, they need something in return?" she asks, avoiding my gaze.

"It's always been that way, I guess?" I say.

"Then why are those people in your life?" she interrupts, giving me no chance to explain. "Seriously, Luke, if I expected anything from you, I would've told you from the start."

"Oh, I know. You've made that perfectly clear," I huff.

"Wait, do you need something from me to feel better or something? Is that what this is about?" She peers toward me, and for a half-second, I fear that she is about to knock my mug of hot chocolate out of my hand.

"Are you serious, Elena? What the hell does that even mean?" I set my mug down on the porch railing before she gets any ideas.

"You know what I mean, don't you? I need to give you something to make you feel worthy of my help. My kindness wasn't enough, right? Well, let me make one thing clear, Luke." She closes the gap between us. "I only wanted your company. That's it."

I take it all in. I wasn't ready to hear that. The invisible wall starts to fade as we remain in an awkward, tense stand-off.

"I'm sorry," I finally say. "This whole situation is just unexpected. *You* were unexpected."

"I feel the same way," she says.

"Listen, I don't want to say anything more that I will end up regretting, but maybe from here on out we just be straightforward with each other?" I smile before realizing that my words would hold me more accountable than her.

Her lips purse. "Can I just say one more thing before we change the subject?"

I nod. "Of course."

"I fully intended to help you write more than one song."

I can feel my heart pounding. On this cold winter night, I start sweating unexpectedly. It feels like my lungs are constricting, as if something is blocking my airways and preventing any air from passing through. Should I tell her now? She needs to know. She must expect something. How could she not? I have to be honest with her. It's only fair.

"Elena, about that song you heard—" I start just as Mr. Madison pokes his head out the front door.

"Elena, it's really cold outside. Why don't you say goodnight to Luke and come inside before you freeze?" he says.

"OK, Dad. I'll be right in," she calls over her shoulder. "Well, I guess I have to go back inside."

I gently withdraw, passing her my mug of hot chocolate. "Thanks for this," I say, gesturing toward the cup. My mind is now torn. I was about to share all my thoughts openly on the porch, but now they retreat back inside of my heart. I grip the railing tightly to steady myself as I get ready to head back home.

"Wait!" Elan calls from her doorway. "What about the song?"

I turn, knowing the moment between us has passed after her dad practically talk-blocked us. "It's nothing." I waved her off. "I was just wondering if you liked it."

"I loved it," she says as the awkward silence returns with a vengeance.

"Thanks," I smile. "You helped me with it."

When I get home, no matter how many times I think about the conversation with Elena, it still doesn't feel any better to me. For the first time in a long while, I want to cry. I hate how this feels. I hate how we have to talk like guarded friends.

I am hiding so much from her, and I can't help but wonder who it will end up hurting more. If everything were out in the open, I'd not only risk unreciprocated feelings, but I couldn't imagine the damage it would do to my friendship with Dax. Dax and I have never fought over a girl before. Better yet, we've barely fought over anything at all.

My heart races as I replay our conversation for the hundredth time. It beats rapidly inside my chest, refusing to accept that I may have to give in. I can't risk losing my best friend over a girl—no matter how strongly I feel for her.

The reality of the situation returns, along with the guilt. I try to push away my feelings and act like they aren't there. I close my eyes for a moment, but when I open them again, I see the image of Elena sitting on my bed.

There she is smiling, mouthing the words, "I wish you had told me how you felt." And just as she reaches for my hand, she disappears because I reach too late.

Chapter Seventeen
1997

It was my first Saturday in a while that I didn't have to work, which was great because I hated the idea of working on Christmas Eve. So, I decided to head to Blockbuster to browse the new releases. I grabbed my keys to the truck after a quick breakfast and headed out the door. Even though I had already finished my Christmas shopping, I wondered if I should buy something for Elena.

Down the street from Blockbuster, there's a used bookstore I thought would be the perfect place to check out. After deciding to rent a few comedies, I drove the two minutes to the store and went inside. The bell above the door rings as soon as it closes behind me.

I walk through the aisles as my fingers slide along the edges of the spines until I find the perfect gift: *Let's Get Invisible*, a *Goosebumps* book I know she's missing from her collection. How I wish she and I could become invisible, and maybe then we could honestly share how we truly feel. Either way, the book is in great condition; it's almost new. So, I grab it along with a bookmark that reads, "I will write books one day." I'm not sure why I pick it up—just a gut feeling.

"Merry Christmas," the young girl behind the counter greets me as I place the items in front of her. "Are any of these items a gift? I can giftwrap them for you," she offers. She's wearing a bright red sweater and matching lipstick. Her earrings are glittery Christmas trees that take up half her lobes.

"Yes, please," I respond. "That would be great."

When I get back home with my bags, I hesitate in the driveway before choosing to walk over to Elena's house. I knock on the door just as Mrs. Madison answers.

"Luke! What a wonderful surprise!" she smiles. "Perfect timing. We are just getting ready to hit the road shortly." Mrs. Madison is also wearing a similar red sweater that I saw the girl at the bookstore wearing. However, instead of earrings, she wears a Christmas tree necklace and a matching barrette.

"Oh," I say. "Where are you spending Christmas?"

"My mother's. She lives an hour from here, so we decided to spend Christmas Eve there. Are you here to see Elena?" she asks.

"Yes," I say. "Oh, and Merry Christmas."

"Merry Christmas to you, too, Luke. Come on in," she ushers me inside.

I take my boots off by the door as Mrs. Madison quickly heads back into the kitchen to finish baking whatever she is bringing to her mother's. Elena surfaces a few minutes later with a couple of sugar cookies. She hesitates for a moment before walking over and hands one to me.

"Thanks, I say.

She guides me into the living room, where we settle on the couch and enjoy our cookies. I glance back at her, feeling her eyes pull me in with all their wonder and mystery. Since we last parted ways, I wasn't sure what to expect the next time I saw her. Gosh, it's so tempting just to lean over and kiss her. She is perfect. Dax was one lucky guy. I just hope he realizes it, too.

She places her hand on my shoulder. Her lips form a half-hearted smile as if they'd rather frown. Either way, she's touching me again. It feels electric. Every hair on my body stands up amid the goosebumps covering me. Goosebumps! I nearly forgot. I reach into one of my bags and hand her the wrapped book.

"What's this?" she asks as she takes the gift into her hands. I notice her nails are painted red.

"It's nothing. Just a little something for Christmas," I reply.

"You got me a Christmas gift?" she looks up at me as she rests it in her lap.

I nodded. Her shoulders press against mine as she tears into the red wrapping, and once she uncovers the book and the bookmark, she grins wider than I've ever seen. "You knew I didn't have this one, didn't you?"

I laugh. "I pay attention."

"And this?" she asks, holding out the bookmark. "What made you pick this one?"

I shrug. I've always seen bookmarks as a way to express yourself. The way you choose to mark your books can say a lot about who you are. "I don't know." I finally say. "I had a feeling one day you would end up writing one."

"I never told you that I wanted to be a writer, but somehow you knew." Her shoulders dropped. "I don't know what to say. This is so unexpected and wonderful."

"You're welcome."

"Dax was here earlier," she says as if I needed to know. "I bought him the new Everclear CD, *So Much for the Afterglow*. Apparently, he already had it. A should have known since you all work at a record store."

"Yeah, he doesn't wait to buy a new album once it hits the shelves—especially since we get a discount."

"I heard," she murmurs.

"What did he get you?" I ask.

She swallows as she tucks her hair behind her ear. "Well, he didn't realize we were exchanging gifts. I guess he thought it was too soon for all of that." She looks down.

"Oh," I say, "Well, Dax is a different species." I try to soften the blow. "I'm sure he didn't mean anything negative by it. Are you OK?"

"Yeah. I'm fine." She continues to look down while fiddling with the sleeve of her sweatshirt.

"Well, I know you have to get going. I hope you have a Merry Christmas, Elena," I say just as I stand up from the couch.

Immediately, her eyes dart toward mine. "Wait!" she exclaims as she stands up as well. "I have something for you, too!" She runs over to her Christmas tree, where she shuffles through the presents.

She hands me a small gift bag and says, "Merry Christmas, Luke."

I take the bag in my hands and remove the tissue paper to reveal a small leather journal. On the front, there's a flower etched into a large stone.

"It's you," she says, pointing to the flower. "Sweet, fragile, yet still as strong as a rock."

"Fragile and strong?" I laugh.

"You are a perfect blend of both." She smiles. "You carry yourself like you have a tough exterior, but I know you're a big softy inside."

"A stoneflower?" I look at her.

"Exactly! I saw it and thought it could help you with your writing, maybe spark a writing revolution of sorts. I want you to fill it with as many songs as you can possibly write." She beams.

"I don't know what to say." I look down at the journal in my hands and then back into her eyes. I wonder if, during moments like these, when we hold each other's gaze, we are aware of the secrets they conceal. Hers are like small crystal oceans, calming me. For a split second, I think I can see tiny waves crashing within them. I imagine myself swimming among those waves.

"This is the nicest gift I think I have ever received." The lingering feeling of her hand on my shoulder fades as I imagine how other parts of my body would respond to her touch. Something in this confusing moment grabs hold of me. I reach out and wrap my arms around her, thanking her once again for the thoughtful gift. Mine definitely paled in comparison.

My body presses against hers, and it feels like we are fitting two pieces of separate puzzles that are desperate to become one. It's like we don't make sense, but somehow we do. We fit. The snow outside the window is falling harder, and all the tears I've been holding back start to gather in my eyes. I do my best to hide them by scratching at my face as if I'm suffering from an allergy attack in the dead of winter. I pull away and thank her once more.

I finally say, "I just don't understand."

"You don't understand what?"

"Why would you do this for me?" I quickly rub my eyes again.

She steps back as I notice the hurt look on her face. "Well, someone once told me that life is too short and that you shouldn't waste it on doing something you didn't love or have passion for."

"But have you ever stopped to think that life is too short to waste it on someone you didn't love or have passion for as well?" The words slip out of my mouth faster than I can stop them. What gave me the right to make such an assumption that was clearly directed toward Dax?

"Are you trying to tell me something, Luke?" she asks the burning question.

"Always," I say.

Chapter Eighteen
Now

"Dude, you've got to be kidding me!" Robbie slaps both of his knees. "She gave you so many hints and opportunities to tell her how you feel, and you didn't freakin' take them! And the journal—" he spins his head around to look back at Monty, too— "That girl liked you! She put more thought into your gift than she did for Dax. It is so painfully obvious that I'm legit secondhand embarrassed. Taylor Swift could easily write an entire album about this."

The clouds have darkened with impending rain as soon as we pull into a gas station. I step out of my truck before the rain starts to pour. Desperate for a snack, we all rush into the store, nearly slipping a few times. Luckily, we catch ourselves before faceplanting into a puddle.

"But what about that Stephanie girl? She came back and apologized. Did you start dating her again?" Robbie asks as soon as he grabs a couple of snacks from the store shelf.

"Against my better judgment, yes. I think I did it more out of retaliation from the whole ordeal with Elena," I admit.

There is no escaping the truth. The weight of reliving it all feels overwhelming, almost suffocating. It traps me, leaving no room to breathe. I no longer feel nervous about where I'm headed. Instead, I'm scared. A strange chaos surrounds my reasons for returning. The world spins around me, and I have no idea which way is up or down. If I could go back in time and change things, maybe I would. It's hard to say. Only knowing what I know now would make time travel worth it. If I didn't have this knowledge, I probably wouldn't change anything.

I head to the restroom and try to dry the rain off my T-shirt with one of those electric hand dryers. Small beads of sweat form on my skin, which I do my best to blot away. The day is warm, but not so hot that it feels like I'm in an oven. It's more of an Easy-Bake Oven feeling. As for the air conditioner in my truck, it's pretty much useless, given its erratic performance and my preference for the breeze.

As I look into the bathroom mirror, my mind drifts back to that distant memory—the one that has the power to break my spirit whenever it surfaces. I see the house. It was framed with beautiful hydrangeas, which scented the air whenever a breeze swept through.

I see myself walking. My steps felt unsteady, as if my legs were made of steel. I had to drag them one by one until I reached the front door, which was recently painted a cherry apple red. To the side of the door was the doorbell that my finger slowly moved toward.

I could hear movement on the other side of the door. I looked in the window and saw he was there. The words he was saying were muffled and distorted, as if I were hearing him talk from underwater.

Then the part of my memory that I have successfully buried in a graveyard of countless others is exhumed…

I look over at a small child who continues to play.

"I will always be here for you. I mean that." His hand rests on Elena's shoulder.

Straightaway, they move closer to where the child is playing. The guy I know to be Dax pulls Elena into an embrace. "Don't worry. You know I love you. You can always count on me."

My finger pulls away from the doorbell and falls to my side as I see him kissing her on the cheek, before they sit down on the sofa without knowing I am just outside.

For a long time, I couldn't remember the memory at all. It would come back in bits and pieces, just like it does today. I could never tell if I had blocked out certain parts to heal, or maybe they had been buried under a pile of forgotten memories that I had collected over the years and never properly sorted through. Still, something, even now, doesn't feel right about the memory. Is it really a memory? Or is it a lie? And, if it is a lie, why would I continue to torture myself with it?

I rejoin Monty and Robbie inside my truck again. Robbie has his phone pressed to his ear.

"I'm not far, Mom," he says into his phone. "Yes, I know. You don't have to remind me every time I talk to you. Jeez. You are so lucky you have me," he goes silent for a moment as if listening to what she had to say in response. "No. Not yet. We are close."

When he hangs up, he startles as if he hadn't seen me sit down.

Traffic on the interstate is jammed. I'm unsure if it's due to an accident or construction, but we've been crawling at 5 mph for the past twenty minutes. Aside from the traffic noise, the truck is quiet. Robbie pretends to play drums on his knees, while Monty looks ready to nod off.

It's strange, but I feel a real connection to this kid. I'm almost living vicariously through his youth and naivety, which makes me wish I could go back in time and do things all over again.

Maybe he was right. Maybe I truly have a tendency for self-sabotage.

Chapter Nineteen
1998

The week after Christmas was a total chaos at the mall. Between shoppers needing to return gifts and those desperate to spend their gift certificates, Darryl kept us all working straight through our entire break from school.

The four of us were also scheduled to work on New Year's Eve before heading to Dax's to practice a little. Our school is hosting a talent show in February for the first time, and Dax thinks it's a great idea to showcase our talent in front of that audience. But I can think of a million other audiences I'd rather perform for than all the jerks in my graduating class.

Monty is behind the counter, talking with Dax when I arrive at the store. He is holding an Everclear CD, which Monty takes from him and places behind the counter. It must be the one Elena bought him for Christmas. I don't blame her for being annoyed. He kept talking about it and then went out and bought it himself.

"Everclear, huh?" I say as if I don't know about the gift.

"Already bought it, but at least now I have some store credit to buy something else," Dax says just as a couple of girls our age walk by the store. They peer in, catching his and Jordan's attention before smiling and waving in their direction.

"Who are they?" I asked, as I pointed toward the girls passing by.

"Just a couple of girls we hung out with over break. We met them at the mall one day and decided to chill," Jordan responds.

"Does Elena know?" I look at Dax.

"Elena? She was busy with her family or something. Why does she need to know anything? It's not like she's my mom. I don't have to report to her," he huffs as he starts browsing the posters on display.

"Well, did anything happen?" I ask.

But just as Monty shakes his head to stop me from reacting, I notice Jordan and Dax winking at each other.

And that was all I needed to know.

It's a new year, but I'm still the same old me. I've decided to start using my new journal to transfer all the songs I wrote about Elena so I can keep writing more whenever the mood strikes. It will be my private sanctuary of feelings, like an entire album dedicated to her.

As for New Year's Eve, it was dull. We practiced for an hour or two before Dax's mom suggested we call it quits after the ball dropped. At Monty's insistence, I didn't bring up the girls from the mall earlier unless I was planning to tell Dax how I really felt. So, I had no choice but to stay silent. I kept my head down and focused on the music, even though I wanted to grab my guitar and smash it over Dax's head.

Now, I'm back home. The kitchen linoleum feels icy beneath my feet. Outside, the temperature is below freezing, and no matter how much we turn up the heat, it still feels like living inside an igloo. I pour myself a cup of coffee and curl up on the couch with a blanket. The warmth flows through me, providing a layer of protection against the cold air.

I think about Dax and those girls again, and how painfully obvious it was that he is not as serious about Elena as I thought (or maybe she thought). But still, it's not my place to interfere with my friend. Then again, she is my friend, too. So, where does my loyalty lie? With her? Or with Dax? I'm caught between a rock and a stoneflower.

My journal sits beside me as I vent into it. But do I truly dare to confess everything to an open book? This wasn't meant to be a diary, yet I'm treating it like one (just a musical version, that is). I have to admit, the more I think about it, the more I see potential for a really good album here. It's a blend of all the feelings I've had since Elena entered my life. It captures the delicate emotions alongside the tougher ones, like unrequited love. It truly reflects the essence of the etching on the front. Elena was right. I will call it "The Stoneflower Revolution."

Then the writing magic happens.

I don't come up for air, not once. My hand refuses to let go of the pen and leave the safety of the paper. With each word, my lyrics come to life as my emotions pour into them. The words come to me as naturally as breathing. I have finally found them, or maybe they've found me. I hold nothing back; it's like confiding in a friend.

The situation begins to tear through my soul like a sharp dagger. It feeds on my denial. It laughs in my face no matter how desperately I try to avoid it. It also creates an unrelenting ache that lingers, as if I have swallowed a lump of bricks settling in the pit of my stomach. Writing helps, but it is only a temporary emotional bandage.

For now, my written words communicate more truth than my lips would ever dare to speak.

When we return to school after break, I pass Stephanie in the hallway. I half-expected her to pretend like she didn't know me, but instead, she smiles and waves like she used to. It was a nice distraction. I missed the feeling of being wanted.

"Maybe you should…" Monty interrupts my thoughts. "It might help get your mind off things."

"No." I shake my head. "There's no way I'm going down that road again. She cheated on me, remember?"

"People make mistakes." He shrugs. "Either way, you can't be pining over a girl your best friend is dating. That is not a good road to travel down either."

I wait until Chemistry class, where I sit a row away from Stephanie, to consider Monty's suggestion. Pinning or rebounding weren't exactly two good options to choose from. Still, I remember how Stephanie looked that day she came over to my house. Was she as remorseful as she seemed? And if people made mistakes, could I really be sure she wouldn't make the same mistake again?

If I gave Stephanie another shot, what would it hurt? I could just break up with her again if necessary. And it would be nice to have an emotional buffer around Elena, even if that might not make me sound like a standup guy.

Either way, I tore a sheet of paper from my notebook and wrote a note to Stephanie, which I handed to her when the teacher wasn't looking.

When she opens it, her eyes widen, and a smile slowly forms on her face.

I guess she didn't have to circle yes.

February arrives faster than Cupid's arrow. The talent show is nearly here, and I'm a bundle of nerves. I felt okay until Chase started cracking jokes at my expense during homeroom that morning. Part of me thinks he's just upset that Stephanie and I are back together, and it has nothing to do with me about to perform with the band on stage.

Yes, Stephanie and I are back together. It's been a nice distraction having her around and someone to talk to, even if it's just surface-level stuff. Stephanie and I have never had a deeper connection, and probably never will.

It wasn't until the last minute of our final band practice that we all agreed on what song to perform. Originally, Dax wanted to do one of the ballad-like songs, thinking it would win over the girls, but the rest of us wanted to rock out. We played as if our lives depended on it because if we were going to showcase our talent, we needed to get everyone excited.

"This is the song we have to perform at the talent show!" Dax says as he skims my notebook because I don't dare let him get his hands on my journal. "'Pivot'. It's genius!"

"You seriously want to perform this song?" I shake my head in disbelief. It was a song I wrote while trying to figure out my situation with Elena and Stephanie.

"Yeah. It's genius. I think it's cool that you used a *Friends* reference."

We set up our equipment on stage and do a quick sound check to make sure everything is working and sounds good. Just before the curtain opens, Dax looks back at us and says, "Do you think they're going to like us?"

"I think there is a slight chance." I wink.

The curtains opened up, revealing a dark auditorium. Besides the first few rows, it's hard to see anyone else's face clearly. I keep my eyes on where Kevin from homeroom is working the spotlight for the stage because I know that the moment I start looking at the audience, I'm going to panic. Or puke.

Our goal was to rock out, and we definitely did. Monty crushed it on drums, Jordan tore it up on bass, and Dax hit notes I don't think he even knew he could while he sang the lyrics to *Pivot*.

The four of us that evening experienced our first taste of "fame" because the crowd loved us. We sounded good. We vibed. We probably have more than a slight chance at making it.

We exited the back of the stage into the hallway outside, where Elena and a few of her friends were waiting to congratulate us on a great performance. Dax was so enthralled by the show and the high-fives being handed out like candy as we all recounted every second of our performance while Elena stood idly by, waiting for him to notice her.

As for me, *I* noticed her. I was about to go to her when Stephanie came rushing down the hallway and threw herself at me. "Luke! You were amazing!" she shouted. She kisses me in front of everyone like I'm a famous rockstar, while I notice out of the corner of my eye that Elena has both of her eyes on Stephanie and me.

"We should go back inside the auditorium to see who wins tonight. There are only a few more acts left until the end," Jordan pipes up.

But just as we are about to turn the corner toward the front entrance of the auditorium, we hear our band's name being called from the front of the stage.

"Our winner tonight is Slight Chance! Come on up here, Luke Grant, Dax Howard, Monty Tennison, and Jordan Baxter! Come get your trophy!"

As if our bodies had taken flight, we glided down one of the aisles and climbed the stage stairs, where Jason, a fellow classmate, held out a trophy that Dax immediately snatched and held up in the air like we had just won an MTV Video Music Award.

Dax also grabs the microphone from Jason and starts his first-ever "Thank you" speech. Neither Monty, Jordan, nor I wanted to give any formal speech to the crowd. We just stood there smiling; however, I couldn't help but imagine that it was Elena who jumped into my arms instead of Stephanie.

That's when I realized that no matter how hard I tried to pivot my feelings away from her, I couldn't seem to keep them there. They were attracted to her—magnetized.

If I were Dax, I would have had her on stage with me. I owe that girl so much and more.

Doesn't he realize that *she* is the trophy?

Chapter Twenty
1998

Time flies by when you're having fun—or if you're working and booking gigs every weekend.

The clouds dispersed, and the sun reappeared, leaving August to end with scorching temperatures. In four days, we will be performing for an A&R representative, also known as a label scout, and Dax believes we should have more songs to choose from than our usual set. I don't dare mention the songs I've written in the journal Elena bought me. They're not meant for the world just yet.

The A&R opportunity came through Darryl and his connections. Apparently, he's in college with a guy who knows someone at the label and helped us out. All we needed to do was agree that Darryl was the best band manager for us and offer him the position. Maybe he has a brighter future after community college.

The rest of the summer passes like a gust of wind. It moves so fast that my junior year almost felt non-existent. Summer plans fell apart, and it was also the first summer on record that we never had a single afternoon to skate. Regarding Auburn itself, people flocked to the lake, transforming our hometown into the perfect summer destination.

Over the past few months, as the song suggested, I focused all my energy on shifting my feelings from Elena to Stephanie. Sometimes, it felt fake, like she was just a placeholder for when the lead was out sick. And although our relationship in the second round seemed better than the first, something still felt missing. And it wasn't her fault.

Whether I pivot or not, Elena crosses my mind so often that she leaves traces of her footprints everywhere. Sometimes, if I'm not watching her closely, she begins to wander down into my heart. When that happens, I do my best to steer her away and keep her confined to my mind. It's bad enough having her there, but it's the lesser of two evils because I have a little more control over her there. But my heart? No, it's far too fragile a place for her to start poking around.

And now, as I'm staring directly into Stephanie's face, it suddenly switches to Elena's. Damn. She's definitely a tough one to shake.

"What time are the guys coming over?" Stephanie asks as she reapplies her lip gloss.

My parents were out running errands when Stephanie stopped by. As soon as I led her inside, she kissed me and tugged on my shirt, pulling me toward my bedroom while kicking off her flip-flops, eager for some time alone. Her tongue tangled with mine as she pulled me onto my bed.

"I'm so happy we are back together," she breathes into the nape of my neck.

"Me, too," I say, keeping my eyes closed because I'm afraid that if I open them, I will see Elena again.

My body eventually relaxes under her touch, and I can feel the tension leaving my stiff limbs. However, her body moves in sync with mine as if she's feeding off my energy. We immediately start shedding our clothes, falling into the awkwardness of two young people exploring each other's bodies for the first time. But this wasn't our first experience. We looked at each other with a new, unfamiliar interest that hadn't been there before.

Our naked embrace guides me toward something unexpected. Our bodies move together like machines—unnatural and stiff. The actions are predictable. The moans of pleasure come on cue. When it's over, I don't feel any more satisfaction than I would from completing a task. As I look down at her, I wonder if she feels the same way.

It's always easy to say the relationship is full of magic until you actually perform a trick.

I kissed her and excused myself as I headed to the bathroom. She doesn't follow; instead, she stays cuddled up in my bed. The rise and fall of her chest fades into the background as I close the door behind me.

Stephanie's perception isn't one of her strong suits. She tends to settle for whatever hurts the least, which I find both admirable and delusional. Based on her behavior, she probably hasn't noticed a change in my emotions. As for me, I feel like I've betrayed my own heart.

I like Stephanie. I really do. But like I said, something is missing, and it's not her fault. Things weren't always like this between us. In the past, there was no comparison. But now, comparisons come easily when there's something (or someone) to compare things to. The past has become nothing more than a painful reminder of how flawed everything is right now. It makes everything hurt even more. Every time I kiss her or say something sweet, there's a sense of emptiness in those actions and words. It's like regifting emotions meant for someone else.

I wouldn't be surprised if Stephanie sensed the disconnect between us. Then again, since she usually chooses the option that would hurt the least, she probably thinks it's nerves about our upcoming show. One thing I do know is missing is that I don't feel safe enough to be my true self around her. Not before. Not now. After my time with Elena, I realized that some people bring out the best in you, including the sides you love and the sides you don't. But it's those people who help you appreciate your whole self, and Elena did that for me. Stephanie is a great person, but sadly, she isn't my person. She unintentionally brings out the sides of me that best suit her.

Honestly, I don't know what my intentions are or how long I plan to keep things going between us. I chose to get back together with her—under false pretenses—and I admit it was a stupid thing to do. I had no intention of hurting her or causing her unnecessary pain, but again, my lack of honesty is the cause of yet another problem in this relationship. Words are too risky now. I just want to understand what I might lose and whether it would even be considered a loss.

I stare at myself in the bathroom mirror. I look down at my arm, where the guys and I all decided to get our band's logo tattooed. So much has changed in such a short time, yet so much has stayed the same. I was branded.

An hour later, the guys head over to my place to review the setlist and narrow down the five songs we will perform in front of the rep. Dax wants to control the opening and closing songs so that the entire set flows together like an album. However, none of us can really focus. We are full of nervous energy over the fact that a simple band like ours might be headed toward our big break. It's something you read about in books and movies, but never in real life.

Yet, this is real life.

Since Darryl decided he couldn't get enough of managing us at the store and wanted to manage us as a band, we all agreed that he had an excellent ear for music as well. He understood what made certain songs succeed more than others. He was certainly opinionated, but his opinions added value. That's why we all decided to leave the setlist selection up to him.

I leave my bedroom to grab a few snacks while the guys go through my notebook for the hundredth time. When I return, Dax is standing in the corner of the room with my leather journal in hand. "What's The Stoneflower Revolution?" he asks, holding it out to me and pointing at the page where I scribbled down the title of what was supposed to be my private collective works.

"It's nothing," I said as I reached for it. "Just give it here."

"No, Luke. It's not *nothing*. You have some amazing songs in here. Why are you holding out on us?" he asks as he begins reading one of the songs out loud, "Goosebumps."

"Well, we are not singing any of them. They are not for the band," I stammer.

"Who are they for then? Another band?" Jordan snickers.

The only person in the room who understands what's going on is Monty. Out of everyone in my life, he is becoming more in tune with my feelings than I am myself. He knows exactly what this journal is full of— even if I've never told him directly.

"Just let it go, Dax," Monty says. "If Luke wanted those songs for the band, then he would have given them to us."

"But they are really good," Dax counters. "They should be for us. We need new material."

And after we spent the next half hour debating over the ownership of my songs, I realized I am no match for Dax's insistence.

He wins again.

It's the night of the show, and we can barely sit still. I'm already sweating profusely. Of all the shows we've done, this one really matters. It's the one we're going to be judged on to see if we have what it takes to succeed. The one that will decide if there's a real chance for Slight Chance.

We're backstage in our dressing room, pumping ourselves up for what we hope will be a successful night. Dax makes us jump around in a circle, just like we used to do before baseball games. Darryl is reviewing all the details and reminding us how important the show is. Even our families came out to support us after we told them about the scout. My mom made T-shirts for everyone to wear—our very first band T-shirts.

We stepped onto the stage and played the five songs we chose with ease. The fifth was "Goosebumps," which Dax was determined to use as the finale. It was originally supposed to be a slower song, but Dax decided to add some more energy. I have to admit, it sounded good, but it wasn't quite how I had envisioned it sounding.

As much as I was soaking in the applause and cheers from the audience, I started to feel a headache coming on. The strings of my guitar blurred against the movement of my fingers until I wasn't even sure if I was hitting the right notes. Thank goodness for muscle memory.

After we finish playing our last song, "Goosebumps," I try my best to hide the emotions spilling out of my eyes, lungs, and heart and rush back into our dressing room. I need something to ease the pounding in my head, which feels like it's trapped in a vise. But just as I get there, I see Elena sitting on the couch with my journal in her hands. I rub my eyes to make sure I'm not dreaming. Is she really here? If she is, I really need to do a better job hiding it from everyone, like I do with my real feelings.

"What is all this?" Elena holds out the journal. "Is this about me—us?" Her eyes plead with me to be honest.

My head is pounding, but my heart is pounding even more. I am desperate for relief. The last thing I expected was this roadblock, but nothing about Elena has ever been predictable. She sits there waiting for me to say something. And, as always, I question whether I am ready to be honest with her. The only difference is that this time, I'm both exhausted and exhilarated after the show, so my guard isn't fully up. So, I let everything out. Timing has never been my strong suit.

"Yes," I confess the one simply word that finally freed my soul.

"You mean to tell me that you have felt this way about me all along?" Her face reddens as her eyes begin to match.

"From the moment I met you," I say, exhaling a deep breath into the space between us. It felt like I had been holding my breath for nearly a year.

"Then why the hell didn't you say something? I thought we weren't hiding things from each other. Why did you lie?" she yells at me. "Why did you keep this from me?"

"Because you started dating my best friend, Elena," I yell back at her. "What the hell was I supposed to do? Confess like some jealous guy who didn't get the girl?"

"That's for me to decide, not you," she snaps. "You have no idea how upset I am with you right now."

"You're upset? Listen," I stammer as the vise tightens even more. "I'm only saying this because it's you, but Dax? Seriously, Elena?"

Her furrowed brow says it all, "What are you talking about, Luke? What is wrong with Dax? He is your best friend, right?"

"Yes, which means I know him better than you." The words spilling from my mouth feel like acid, burning my tongue and everything else they touch. "Like every other girl, you fall for his looks and charm. He's great, don't get me wrong, but he doesn't want a commitment—at least, not a real one."

"Really?" she folds her arms across her chest. "And you can speak to what he wants?"

"I just know you deserve better," I say.

And now you're an expert on that, too. Wow, Luke, I never knew you knew so much about other people," she peers over at me. "So, if you knew what was better for me, then why didn't you—" she stops herself— "You know what?" She gets up from the dressing room couch. "Never mind. Forget everything." She tosses the journal onto the floor.

"What, Elena? Just say it," I say. "Open and honest, right?"

She shakes her head as if she's moments away from releasing the tears she's been holding back.

"Where is the passion, Elena? Where is the spark between you two? How can you spend your time with someone who doesn't go to the ends of the earth to sweep you off your feet? You deserve so much more than what you're settling for." My words continue to burn through everything they touch.

"I could say the same thing about you," she says. "No wonder you struggle with your writing. You have no idea how to be vulnerable and honest."

Where is all of this coming from? And where are the damn painkillers? I finally find one, hoping some of its effects will reach my heart. Just as I look up at her, we've become nothing more than reflections of each other: two people choosing the options that hurt less. In that case, I was no different than Stephanie.

"You don't know what it's like to really love someone, do you?" I sigh.

"Just stop it, Luke." She begins sobbing. "How dare you assume what I do or don't know about love. You don't know everything. Nor can you be so loud about something you have spent months being silent about!"

My mouth snaps shut. But by the time her words sink in, she's already walking away. She doesn't care if I have anything to say in response. She was done.

Without thinking, I move toward her and pull her into my arms. My body presses against hers, with only our tears seeming to keep us apart. I lean down and lift her chin to meet mine. My lips find hers instinctively, as if guided by an unseen map. When they meet, they sink into each other as if they've finally come home. I kissed her the way I wish I had from the moment I met her.

I'm tasting her tears, and she's tasting mine. I breathe in the scent of her skin and can't pull away. It's everything I ever imagined. But as she keeps kissing me, I realize something: this feels simple. It feels right. There's nothing forced between us.

My hand cups the back of her head, pulling her closer as if I want us to become one. My other hand explores whatever it can, and I hope I never wash these hands again.

When we finally catch our breath, I glance back at her in disbelief. Did my headache cause a lucid dream? Or is this actually happening? Our tear-streaked faces reveal how stunned we are, as if we don't know how to process what just took place.

"I can't believe this just happened," she finally says.

"Elena, I feel for you in ways I know he doesn't," I reply, kissing her once more.

But before any more words are exchanged between us, a voice unexpectedly appears in the doorway, "Oh, yeah? In what way is that?"

Chapter Twenty-One
1998

Between Dax witnessing my interaction with Elena, and Elena darting out of the dressing room before anyone could say anything, I know things are not going to be good for me. The pain in my head worsens.

By all accounts (all of which are well deserved), Dax is furious. As he yells at me, all I can think about are two things: kissing Elena and how she kissed me back. This wasn't a forced kiss without reciprocation. SHE KISSED ME. She meant that kiss just as much as I did.

Still, I knowingly allowed my best friend's girlfriend, the love of my life, to press her lips against mine. I allowed myself to get so lost in the moment that I didn't stop to think about the repercussions for my actions. I enjoyed every second of it, and sadly, I would probably do it all over again. Right, wrong, or indifferent.

Dax throws every name he can at me, and rightfully so. Even though I agreed with everything he was saying, I hated all the name-calling. From the depths of my soul, I HATED IT. Why not get straight to the point? Why not address why you're so angry instead of adding all that fluff? And no matter what I tried saying in response, nothing softened the blow he took tonight. We left the stage feeling high above the clouds, only to both come crashing down to the jagged earth instead.

He kicks one of the dressing room chairs just as Monty, Jordan, and Darryl rush in to see what all the fuss is about. "I can't fucking believe you, Luke!" he yells.

"I'm sorry, Dax, but if you would let me explain," I start, but just as I was trying to get the words out, Dax's fist comes flying into my jaw. He connects with excruciating force, causing him to double back and fall to the floor.

"What the hell is going on here?" Darryl yells while trying to keep his voice down. "That A&R guy is coming in here any minute, and if he sees you all acting like fools, there's no way you're getting signed. Don't screw this up!"

Dax is burning red. His chest rises and falls as if he just finished a marathon, while I stay on the floor, holding my face. The argument was bound to happen, but I never thought it would unfold like this. We've always respected each other, but that all fell apart when I finally shared my feelings. Again, timing has never been my strong suit.

I spent the next twenty minutes explaining to the guys what happened after Darryl followed Dax out of the room to calm him down.

"You kissed her?" Monty's jaw drops. "Dude…"

"I know. I know. I didn't realize he was standing right outside the door," I say.

"Yeah, but that shouldn't be the reason you're sorry. You're mainly just apologizing for getting caught, not for kissing her," Jordan replies.

"Honestly, yeah. Besides, I have been in love with her since the moment I met her. I was just too stupid not to say anything," I sigh.

"Then you missed your chance," Jordan interrupts again. "If you didn't have the guts to be straightforward with Dax from the start, then you don't get to step in whenever you feel ready to."

"Fair," I admit. "I never intended to hurt anyone."

When Darryl finally returns with Dax in tow, we all wait in tense silence until the A&R guy arrives. As he talks and critiques our act, I stay closed off, not hearing a single word he says. Dax avoids eye contact with me at all costs. When the rep, Kenny, says he sees promise in us and wants to consider a conditional contract, everyone jumps in the air as if we just won the lottery. The excitement masks the tension between Dax and me, but we are still aware of that exists.

After Kenny leaves, Darryl analyzes everything he said. Dax, however, walks out without even saying goodbye to any of us. When I get home, I call Elena, but she doesn't answer the phone. I see her bedroom light on, but her parents tell me she is asleep. Is she avoiding me? If she is, then why? Suddenly, I am unsure of what to think or feel. Did I just lose two of the most important people in my life?

For the rest of the night, I decide that maybe she's trying to process everything just like I need to. Still, I wish she would talk to me. I need her more than she realizes. I don't bother calling Dax because I know he needs time to cool off. But by the next afternoon, I tried to reach him. Even his mother hinted at the rift between us, but he didn't

answer the phone either. I have no choice but to face him the next time I see him. So, I grab a bag of ice and tend to the only wound I can heal.

The clouds are dark and heavy, hanging over me and showing no signs of moving. The weather forecast said we might get some thunderstorms this Labor Day weekend, which could potentially ruin anyone's plans for a nice picnic. I barely leave my room, so it doesn't matter much to me. However, I had a shift at Record City tonight, and it would be too late to call in. I had been dreading this day for over a week, knowing I'd have to face Dax. If I've learned anything from this experience, it's that facing it now is better than putting it off.

There was a strange silence in the store when I arrived. Dax was talking to Darryl, but he immediately stopped as soon as he saw me walk in. The tension in the room was thick, and the last thing I wanted was to get into another argument with Dax. My heart and jaw couldn't handle it.

"I will leave you both to figure this out," Darrly says, looking at us both. "In case you weren't aware, you have a huge opportunity presented to you that not many people get, and I would hate to see you ruin it because you can't get along."

"Getting along wasn't the issue," Dax huffed.

"Well, figure it out," Darryl orders. "But if a customer comes in, I better not see you smashing each other into the displays."

Dax rocks back and forth on his heels before glancing back at Darryl. Darryl is in the back of the store rummaging through boxes and banging around as if he doesn't realize how loud he's being. I lean against the counter, trying to figure out what to say or who should speak next. I fumble with my nametag and stare at the clock, hoping it will hurry up.

But Dax still remains silent. He doesn't even act like we're sharing the same space. I know he has every right to be mad at me because I'm angry at myself for hurting him.

"Nice face," he finally says, referring to the bruise decorating my chin.

"Dax, I'm sorry," I say, ignoring his comment.

"You're sorry?" he scoffs. "Wow, thank you! I feel so much better now." He places his hand on his chest as if to mock my apology.

The details of my kiss with Elena remain at the forefront of my mind as if they purchased prime real estate and have no plans to sell. Every time I think about that moment, I am overwhelmed by it, like a wave washing over me and pulling me underwater, where I feel like I'm drowning. My body reacts as if I still remember how her strawberry Lip Smacker lips tasted. Just one kiss, and I'm hooked on her like a drug. The passion between us was undeniable, which is how I knew she kept her feelings from me, too.

Dax begins, "I saw you kiss her."

I nod because it makes no sense to deny anything.

"And she kissed you back," he continues, as if we need to recount everything beat by beat.

"Dax, I'm—" I begin to say, but he raises his hand to stop me.

"Since that night, I keep replaying every kiss I had with Elena in my mind, wondering if we ever kissed the way I saw you two do. And I'm just so pissed off at you for having this intense moment with my girlfriend, and I can't even remember one time she and I experienced something similar," he explains to me.

"Dax, I should have been honest with you from the start. I just didn't think you two would end up together. You are both so different, and I was just being ignorant," I say.

"I wish you'd told me, but you didn't — and that's your fault. Which means, the whole time she and I have been dating, you've been secretly in love with her. Wait, not so secret anymore, because you've been writing about your feelings for her in our songs, which I've been singing like some fool," he sneers.

"I know," I say, agreeing. "I'm sorry for everything."

"And what about Stephanie?" he asks. "Are you two still together?"

"Yeah," I admit. "I'm not proud of the circumstances."

Both Stephanie's and Elena's eyes come into focus. I imagine them both staring at me, but it's clear which one I am looking back into. No one in my entire life, past or present, has ever looked at me the way Elena does. I miss her smile—the gentle, warm, and inviting smile that gives me comfort and compassion. And those lips… she kissed me as if she had waited lifetimes to do it. We are not so different, she and I.

The only thing I gained from her pulling away from me is that I've been able to see things clearly. It gave me time to figure things out and maybe end the confusion that's been haunting me like a persistent shadow. But how do you tell someone how much you love them? Would I even be allowed to be that honest?

I try to tell Dax that I wasn't trying to hide secrets from him, but everything spiraled out of control. The longer it went on, the harder it became to be honest.

"The truth always comes out in the end," Dax says.

He is right because it always happens—and it did. But before either of us can say anything more, customers start flooding into the store, and we have no choice but to get back to work. It isn't until closing time that we get a chance to talk some more.

It's after midnight when we finally leave the mall. As soon as we reach the main doors, the wind is tearing through us from every direction. Even the rain is so heavy that it's falling sideways, soaking us to the bone.

"It's like a fucking tornado!" Dax yells at me as I hold onto the railing outside, making my way down the stairs. I have a feeling that if I let go, I might fly away.

"Seriously! How the hell are we supposed to get to our cars? Should we even try to drive in this?" I yell back.

"Well, we can't stay here! The mall is locked," he screams into the wind.

We decided on the count of three that we would book it for our vehicles. Then, once safely inside, I would follow him to his house since it was the closest.

Just as I buckle my seatbelt and start my truck, the wind is blowing even harder. Debris is flying everywhere and hitting my windshield, making it hard to see anything ahead. Even my wipers are moments from tearing off.

Dax is ahead of me, and I slowly follow him as best as I can. We make it out of the mall and turn onto the first side street, where he swerves out of nowhere. I can't tell what caused him to do that until I look out my driver's side window, and all of a sudden it becomes clear.

Then, all goes black.

Chapter Twenty-Two
1998

I don't know what day it is. Sometimes, I wake up randomly, glance at the clock on the wall as if it matters, then fall back asleep only to wake up and do the same thing all over again.

"Hey, you." My mom reaches over and pats my knee, which is hidden under a white blanket. "How are you feeling?"

"I don't know." I rub my eyes. "How should I feel?

"Well, you were in an accident," my mom continues. "You were driving through a pretty bad storm we had on Labor Day after you left work, and a big tree fell. Dax was able to avoid it, but you hit it head-on."

I'm overwhelmed by a crushing feeling as I try to remember that night. "Is Dax OK?"

"Dax is okay, sweetheart. He called 911 and stayed with you until the ambulance arrived. He's been coming to see you ever since."

"Wait," I start. "How long have I been here?" I try to sit up in bed but find it too difficult. The room begins to spin, so I slowly lie back down.

"About a month. You missed the start of your senior year, but don't worry — you can still catch up and graduate on time. Your principal doesn't think it will be an issue," she explains.

"This is all too much," I say. "I don't remember a storm or driving in one. Why can't I remember it?"

"Well, you hit your head pretty bad, and the doctor said that we should expect some memory loss. They don't know if it will be permanent or temporary, or even how much of your memory would be affected because you haven't been awake long enough for them to run tests on you," she says.

My head throbs as I try to recall any memory—even a crumb—but there's nothing. I feel frustrated. The more I try to remember, the more overwhelmed I get. It fills the hospital room like I'm dodging grenades.

"Is Dax here now?" I ask, hoping he can help fill in the blanks.

"No. I didn't want a lot of visitors to disturb you, so we limited how many people we allowed to come," she answers. "But I did bring you a couple of things from home in case you woke up and were feeling up to it." Mom reaches into her bag and retrieves my CD book and Discman. Then, she hands me a couple of notebooks and a leather journal.

"What's this?" I ask, holding the journal in my hands. I flip through a few pages, puzzled.

"You don't remember this?" She looks at me and back at Frank, who just walked into the room with coffee.

"Hey, kiddo," Frank smiles. "What doesn't he remember?" He turns toward my mom.

"This," she points to the leather journal I'm still holding.

"Do you remember that you and the guys started a band?"

"Oh, yeah. I believe so. Are we any good?"

"You were signed to a label," Frank replies. "We found out it was official after the accident."

"We did?" I ask both of them in disbelief. Dax's crazy idea actually worked.

"You did, sweetie. But try to get some rest. I'm sure the memories will come back to you before you know it." She smiles, but I notice a hint of concern in the way the corners of her mouth don't lift as high as they usually do.

That I can remember.

I'm stuck in the hospital for another week, but I refuse any visitors. When I finally get out, I head home, taking in my surroundings as if I'm seeing everything for the first time. However, as soon as I see Wilson, I realize exactly where I am. My room feels familiar—a safe space where I shut myself off until I'm ready to start putting the rest of the pieces together.

Some moments come back to me in flashes of light. I feel like I'm living in that Céline Dion song, wishing everything could come back to me now. For some reason, vivid memories of my mother playing that song on repeat in the early '90s are enough to have the words burned into my mind, so as much as I hate that I'm suffering from a bit of memory loss, I wouldn't mind forgetting the words.

Luckily, as bits and pieces come back to me, I notice that larger chunks are still missing. It feels like reading a book and getting interrupted mid-chapter. Often, I look through my leather journal and other song notebooks searching for clues. I remember writing some of the songs, but not all of them. Every time I try to create something new, my mind goes blank. My emotions do, too. I don't know what I'm feeling aside from this strange emptiness that I don't know how to fill. What if I'm not recalling something painful? Would it be better to stay in the dark?

In true Luke fashion, I try to process my feelings through writing. I choose to use the leather journal instead of my notebook because I feel more connected to it. My pen lingers on the next blank page, waiting for something to happen.

I feel something, but I'm not sure what. Am I sad? It's hard to tell. *Angry?* No, that doesn't feel right. *Confused?* Yeah, obviously. Then, something strange happens. A rush of emotion starts flooding out of me. There's no clear meaning to what I'm feeling, but they're there, and they want to be noticed.

I don't want them to stop. I don't want to risk losing everything I've bottled inside, especially if it helps me create a clearer picture. My pen moves in a way that the sweeping of ink between the lines almost feels rhythmic. A melody that builds depth and understanding, like a song that needs to be sung.

By now, the sun is setting, which is my only sign of passing time. The faint glow from the remaining daylight filters through my bedroom window, providing enough light until I have no choice but to turn on a lamp. As I keep filling the pages with words, there is a knock on my door.

"Hold on," I say without looking up from my journal. I can't remember how long I've been in this position, hovering over it as if protecting it from rain. My body aches, but my mind feels a small bit of relief. I could keep this going until my hands bleed.

The door finally opens, revealing Dax on the other side.

"Hey, man!" I say as he walks into my room. "I don't remember if we have enough music yet, but I've been writing up a storm. I also found a bunch of songs in this journal and another notebook."

He nods. "Yeah, we have enough for now. We just don't use the songs in that one."

"Why? They're really good. I'm actually impressed that I wrote them," I say, shaking my head in disbelief. "I did write them, right?"

"Oh, yeah, you wrote them," he says. "By the way, how are you feeling?" He steps further into the room, his movements cautious, as if he's trying to avoid any cracks or holes that might trip him up.

"I'm feeling better. Still trying to piece things together," I reply. "I'm glad you're OK, though."

"What is the last thing you remember?" he asks.

I set my pen down, thinking. What's the last thing I remember? I catch glimpses of us at Record City. I see us playing in front of a few crowds. "My parents said we were signed?"

"Yeah, we're just waiting for your signature to get everything in order. There's no rush, though. The label knows you had a car accident," he says. "Is that all you remember?" His eyes look heavy with concern.

"Everything is still a blur," I say. "I'm still trying to work this out." My attention shifts back to my journal.

"Dude, you've had your face buried in that damn book the whole time I've been standing here," Dax says before yanking the journal away from me. My pen slides across the page, and I can see the line it made when Dax holds it up in the air.

"What the hell are you even writing about? Do you even know?" He looks at me. Fury sweeps through the room like a gust of wind. *Wind.* I see rain falling sideways and debris flying all around. Am I remembering?

"Hey!" I yell. "Give it back. I was on a roll, man!" I jump off my bed and try to snatch it from him, but he dangles it above my head. "Knock it off, Dax. What are you, five?" I say as I jump up and down, acting like we're two kids playing a silly game.

Then, once I pull the journal from his tight grip, something inside me shatters. We are furious with each other. And this isn't fresh anger; it's been building for a while. There is pain. There is guilt. There is regret. But why?

In response, Dax shakes his head as if I've disappointed him. *Again?* "You have no idea that you and I have been in a fight, do you? Or why I've been so upset with you?"

I glance at him. My eyes penetrate through him as if attempting to uncover the truth.

"Elena?" Dax looks at me. "Ring a bell?"

I sit down on the edge of my bed. Elena. *Elena?* Oh, my goodness, he knows. But just as I start to follow that train of thought, everything I had forgotten unravels into a mess at my feet.

"You were my best friend, Luke. I trusted you more than anyone else. Why did you do it? Better yet, how could you have done it?" He looks at me, begging for answers that I'm not in the right state of mind to give. "I just need to know, do you love her?"

I can barely remember the whole incident. But I just realized that my heart isn't suffering the same memory loss as my mind. I can still feel love even if I don't clearly remember the event he's talking about. "Something tells me that I do," I say.

"I thought you would say that," he says to me. "Well, I'm glad you're feeling better. I did miss you despite all this shit." He makes his way toward my bedroom door, unaware of how much this small moment has affected me. I am discouraged because I don't know how to fix whatever Dax is talking about. Something happened between me and Elena. But what? I'm still blindly walking through a fog, hoping for the skies to clear, and it's obvious he's not about to help me either.

"Do you hate me?" I ask, stopping him at the door. "For whatever happened, do you hate me?"

"I don't hate you. But we are still together."

"Who?

"Elena and I."

When the weekend finally ends, I head back to school the next Monday, ready to start my senior year. But since I haven't seen anyone except Dax, it's hard to know how everyone will react when they see me.

I try pulling myself together. My eyes are slightly puffy from lack of sleep, and no matter how many times I splash water on my face, I still look hungover.

I haven't driven since the accident because my stepdad took my truck to a body shop, where it's been getting the necessary repairs, so I'm relying on everyone else to give me rides.

After I chug a much-needed cup of coffee, there is a knock on my door. It's Stephanie.

"Babe," she says as soon as I open the door. "I've been so worried about you. Your mom asked everyone to give you space, but it was really hard for me. You don't know how many times I wanted to drive over or call you. I did come to the hospital once, though. Did she tell you?" She reaches over and pulls me in for a hug. Her embrace is warm. "I hope you don't think I'm a terrible girlfriend for not being there."

"No," I reassure her. "You just listened to what my parents thought was best. So, thank you."

She walks into my house, and we sit on the couch. Stephanie wastes no time catching me up on everything I missed at school. I want to ask her why Dax is so upset with me, but it's clear that my relationship with her doesn't often extend into the one I have with my friends.

"Did you hear we got signed? Slight Chance is about to be signed to a label," I tell her.

"Yeah, I heard through the grapevine. How lucky am I to be dating a rockstar?" She winks at me. "But can I ask you something—that is, if you are up to it?"

"Shoot."

I watch as her smile fades from her face. She tucks her hair behind her ears, avoiding eye contact with me. "While you were recovering, I heard some things. I don't know if they were just rumors, but I wanted to ask you first before I believed anything."

"What rumors?" I ask.

"About you," she says, a worried look crossing her face. "And please don't lie to me. The truth always comes out in the end."

"So, I've heard," I chuckle unintentionally. The last person who should be consulting me on telling the truth is her. She once cheated on me in the past and refused to be honest about it—even when I caught her in the act. That's something I haven't forgotten.

"I don't think it's funny, Luke. Did you hook up with Dax's girlfriend?" Her eyes peer at me with laser focus, as though examining how truthful I plan to be. Her body hangs over the couch, as if bracing for an answer she doesn't want to hear.

I don't know what to say to her. It would clearly explain why Dax is so angry at me. A knot forms in my stomach that I can't seem to untie.

"I thought so," she says without waiting any longer for me to respond. "I guess I deserve it, considering I had done it to you." She clears her throat while struggling to stay quiet. "I tried convincing myself that nothing could have happened, even though I had some doubts. I believed you over the rumors because I thought this second chance was stronger than our first."

"Stephanie, I don't know what to say. Unfortunately, I can't answer this. And it's not because I don't want to, I just can't remember."

"I know. You were in a really bad accident. You hit that tree head-on. I heard that if it wasn't for Dax being there, you probably would have been stuck in your truck for who knows how long. You needed medical attention right away, and he made sure 911 arrived as soon as possible," she explains.

Even though she provided the details of the accident, I still don't remember it. Not the wind. Not the tree. Not the crash.

"Yeah, I don't remember that either." I lean back on the couch. "I'm sorry."

"Does it matter?" She stands up from the couch. "Your heart should be a pretty clear indicator of how you feel, at least."

My body sinks further into the couch until I can't move anymore. I can't even look at her. She's right. I never thought I'd say those words. I'm afraid that the longer we sit here, the more the truth might come out in a way neither of us is emotionally prepared for.

"When's the last time you saw her?" she asks. She twirls a strand of her hair. Her nail polish is glitter, matching a similar shade on her eyelids. She shimmers in whichever light filters into the room.

"I'm not sure," I sigh, knowing I'm hurting more people than I ever intended to. Then, just as I'm about to say something, I stop. An image of Elena's face flashes into my mind. She is crying. I suddenly find myself staring into her eyes, losing myself in them. I want nothing more than to take away whatever is causing her sadness. We exchange words. At first, they sound distorted, as if

I am listening to them on a different frequency. Soon, they come through clearly, as if a channel has shifted. I can feel her breath on my skin and her arms wrapped tightly around me. I lean down and kiss her. I can still taste her.

"You just remembered." Stephanie bows her head. "It's written all over your face, and it seems like I'm the only one who can read the encryption."

Chapter Twenty-Three
1998

My first day back at school moves at a glacier's pace. Not only is it my first day back at school, but it's also my first day back at work. My parents thought I was jumping into things too quickly, but I just wanted everything to go back to normal (whatever normal was).

It's great to see everyone and catch up with the guys. Unfortunately, the excitement of being signed to a label isn't enough to erase the awkwardness that's choking us from inside our tiny bubble. At lunch, I barely touch my food while they talk about our music and upcoming gigs. The band was starting to get attention in the media, and before we knew it, we had become local celebrities. Fame was never something I ever aimed for, so I couldn't care less about that part. Still, it was exciting nonetheless.

Dax seems fine to me, but I doubt everything is completely okay between us. The main issue has become the elephant in the room that we are all learning to accept like another member of our band—at least, for now. I understand it sucks that we both have feelings for the same girl, but based on what Dax told me in my room that day, she clearly made her choice. That decision has caused a rift between Dax and me, and a divide between Elena and me as well. I was never very emotional, but she brought out a side of me I never knew existed. My tears have long stained my pillowcase, and I hate feeling so heartbroken with no one to confide in.

Through my writing, I have learned that being heartsick involves small, subtle cracks meant to trip us up in the game of love. They cause feelings of doubt that make you hesitate. In contrast, being heartbroken is a completely different story. It consists of tiny, insignificant fractures that can lead to a heart's total collapse—a heartbreak of epic proportions. It happens when you feel so confident in yourself and your feelings, it's blindsiding because you never see the cracks forming. It trips you up when you never see anything in your way. It's the worst.

However, when it comes to matters of the heart, I have no choice but to cling to what I can remember and what I can still feel.

I head home after school to prepare for my shift and a band meeting that Dax wants to have later tonight. The grass is overgrown because Frank has been working crazy hours, and I haven't been able to help since my accident. The weeds are almost touching the surface of the driveway, and the shrubs are completely out of control. The previous neighbors would definitely have had something to complain about.

Since I have about an hour free, I decide to work on whatever I can.

The sun gives a false sense of happiness that I reluctantly accept. But as my new best friend Céline Dion said, "There were days when the sun was so cruel." Was it cruel? Have my tears turned to dust?

When days are nice like this, everything often feels better, so I allow myself to enjoy the illusion. I know how silly that is because that's exactly what it is: silly. It's foolish to think that someone's life gets better just because the sun is shining overhead like a beacon of happiness. Yet here I am, believing in it. As much as I want to think that everything is sunshine and roses (not weeds), I realize there's a darkness lurking that I can't see. It's the memory of what happened between Elena and me.

I conjure up whatever fragments I'm lucky enough to receive. It's like desperately trying to remember a good dream when morning comes and washes it all away. Thoughts flow through my veins, and as much as they should hurt me for their existence, they excite me instead. My lips burn. My skin feels electrified. My sensory memory seems more reliable than my mind's. Yet, I haven't seen her since everything happened, which has only made my heart ache more. Not that it matters. She chose Dax. Not me.

I'm about to start mowing when she walks out the front door of her house. I can hear her shoes shuffle on the pavement as she begins walking toward me. I can't look directly at her. It's like staring straight at the sun, and I have nothing to shield my eyes from it.

When she's a few feet from me, the mower suddenly roars to life. Her hands are on her hips, as if she's about to scold me.

"What? I look up at her. She starts to speak, but I can't hear anything she is saying over the mower unless she shouts.

"Can you turn that off?" she yells.

"What do you want?" I ask once the mower turns off.

"I wanted to say hi," she says. "It's been a while."

"A while?" I look at her.

"I was going to say a long time," she sighs. "How are you feeling?"

"I'm better. Thanks." I shove my hands into my jeans pockets.

"I know we haven't spoken since everything…" Her words trail off as if she expects me to follow them to their destination. "But I wanted to tell you that I'm sorry."

"Don't apologize. I wouldn't even know what you're trying to apologize for—at least, not entirely." I shrug. The last thing I needed was for her to see how heartbroken I felt inside. It was obvious she now knows how I feel. And it's even more obvious that she still chose Dax despite that.

I stare up at the beacon of happiness, silently praying that things could have been different—that I would have woken up in the hospital with her beside me—because she never left. Damn it, I love this girl. There is no doubt in my heart or mind that whatever happened between us, she must have shared the same feelings. And if that's the case, why aren't we together? Why would she choose him over me?

Dax is my best friend, but we're complete opposites. His love of literature only extends to reading the backs of cereal boxes. He's never enjoyed reading, nor has he ever tried, for that matter. Would he try for her? Elena and I can talk about books for hours.

She wants to be a writer someday; after all, would he even know how best to support her?

Even our sense of humor is more in sync. We laugh at the most ridiculous things, which he often finds corny. *Dumb and Dumber* is one of our favorite movies. We laugh at the same scenes and quote the movie whenever we're in the same room. Dax often joins in, but it's not quite the same because he can't fully appreciate the genius of Jim Carrey.

It's not that he's doing anything wrong; it's just that sharing something with someone makes it feel special. It's a vibe you can't force or create. It's natural like breathing.

The sky no longer looks blue. The sun isn't as bright anymore. Nor is the grass as green as it used to be. It feels like the universe is telling me that without her, nothing is as beautiful. I get it, Universe. It's a *Total Eclipse of the Heart*.

She says to me, "You look sad."

"I'm fine. I just thought I'd help mow the lawn since my stepdad has been working a lot, and my mom isn't really into yard work."

"Yeah." She nods. "You know, this is stupid, Luke. We are talking to each other like we are strangers. I mean, we talked more on the first day we met than we are right now. Come sit down with me," she instructs as she pulls me toward her porch.

"I really can't." I point to the overgrown grass. Yet, she dismisses what I said as she keeps dragging me next door.

"Sit," she motions to the settee.

I sit, but she doesn't say anything, which really isn't much different from when we were standing in my yard.

"You know," she begins, "everything you wrote was beautiful. I had no idea you had felt that way."

I look at her. "Is this the leather journal?"

"Yeah," she responds. "I bought it for you for Christmas." A layer of moisture gathers in her eyes.

"Are you OK?" I ask.

She looks at me as the wetness turns into tiny droplets rolling down her face. I instinctively reach over and wipe them away.

"I know you're still with Dax," I tell her. No point ignoring our own elephant in the room. Apparently, there are plenty of them to go around.

"He told you?" She wipes away a few stray tears.

"Yeah," I say. "I'm just having a hard time putting everything together."

"It's my fault. I came to see you at the hospital, and when you woke up, you—" she stops herself.

"I what?" I ask.

"You called me Stephanie. Everything else you said didn't make much sense, but you kept calling me her name even after I told you who I was. I was hurt, so I just ran out of there and back to him. I think it must have upset you because your mom blocked visitors from that point on."

"I don't remember that."

"Dax told me that your mother mentioned something about memory loss and that they weren't sure how much you'd remember again, so I was worried that if you didn't remember who I was, then you wouldn't remember how you felt," she explains.

"So, basically, you were afraid of being alone. Seriously?" I run my hand over my face. I don't even want to ask her anything else because the details no longer matter. The fact that she and Dax are back together is all I need to know. Yet, my mind tells me I need to know more right now. It all just came back to me now.

I remember.

Elena entered my life when I wasn't aware of how much I needed someone like her. She revealed everything I never knew was missing. The simple things that make a person feel wanted and loved, she gave to me. She brings out a side of me I never knew existed. It's a connection I've cherished from the start. No words to any song can fully express my love for her. Yet, I now have to accept her as only a friend. So, if that's what I must do to keep her in my life, then that's what I will do. After all, that's love.

As we remain seated, I want to cry with her. I hate how things have turned out, but I'm at least glad that everything is now out in the open. Nothing is hidden, and there are no more secrets between us. However, I have a nagging suspicion that she's still hiding something. Something behind her eyes tells me she wants to say more, but she can't—or won't—who's to say?

"Just so you know," I say as I stand up from my seat. "I don't regret a single thing."

"But I thought you didn't remember?" Her eyes widen like tiny saucers.

"I do now. It all just came back to me. Sometimes, memories trickle in. Other times, it's like a burst pipe. I just think that this is all too confusing for us to apologize our way through it. At least, you have nothing to apologize for." I make my way down her porch steps. A few raindrops hit my skin. They cool my arm against the warm air. But when I look back up toward that beacon of happiness, it's no longer there. How ominous. How fitting.

"I hope Dax realizes how lucky he is," I say, turning back around. My heart races, but it slows its rhythm, knowing there's nothing to race toward. There is no finish line.

She looks back at me, and the confusion grows ten times worse. It squeezes my heart, and I realize the only way to free it is to understand why she truly picked him over me. It couldn't be the whole story.

This girl doesn't realize how deeply I've fallen for her. It would take countless lifetimes for me to rebuild myself. The reasons I fell in love with her are the same reasons I am now utterly broken. My heart has completely shattered. Tiny, insignificant fractures.

I wish I could forget it all.

Later at work, my eyes feel weak and tired. I still get occasional bouts of fatigue and headaches, but I've been told they will eventually fade with time. My body feels like Jell-O as it molds into the chair I'm sitting on behind the counter while Darryl reviews the contract in more detail. All I can think about is my conversation with Elena.

When the meeting ends, Dax says he's going to meet up with her, while Monty and I stay behind to finish our shift.

"We will meet up later for another quick band rehearsal, OK?" Dax says to us before he leaves.

Monty and I get a couple of late dinners at the food court a few hours later. We sit down as the steam from our pizza rises around us like a cheesy, saucy-smelling cloud.

"My mom made us some cookies." Monty reaches into his bag and pulls out a small container. "Chocolate chip. I told her they were your favorite."

"Yep. I literally devour them every time she makes them." I smile.

"How is everything going?" He blows on his pizza before taking a bite.

"It's going," I say. "Not that I have any control over anything."

Monty nods his head as if he understands what I'm trying to say.

"I've always believed that if you wanted something badly enough, you'll do whatever it takes to get it," I say.

"Well, yeah," he says. "That's why they are called dreams, because not everyone has what it takes to make them come true, but everyone has what it takes to dream."

"I suppose." I take a bite of my pizza. "Can I ask you something?"

"Of course, dude."

"What if the thing you really want comes at a cost?"

"Well, I guess you have to decide if it's a price you're willing to pay," he says.

"I think I got a taste of that already," I smirk, even though it's not one bit funny.

"If it makes you feel any better, I heard what happened. Well, you told me, but honestly, I'm just as confused about everything as you are," he says.

"What do you mean?" I ask.

"I'm not saying what you did was right, but regardless of the situation, there was something there—a spark. I never saw that with them."

After we eat, I stay behind for a few minutes so I could write. I decided that if I ever had the chance to make an album my way, I would indulge in performing these songs. However, they would never become the property of the bands. I could never go on stage and have Dax sing what isn't his to sing like some puppet. The songs are mine. Well, they are hers. They will never belong to him.

I turned to the front of the journal and wrote these words:

She fills the silence and emptiness that aches within my soul.
She fills it without effort.
She fills it without gain.
She fills it with her eyes, burning a thousand lifetimes into mine. In each one, we are together. There are no obstacles to overcome. No one is standing in our way.
She is gentle yet strong. She displays these qualities in me as well.
She is tough as stone.
She is as fragile as a flower.
She is my revolution.
I will never stop fighting for her, even if it seems like I've laid down my sword.

It wasn't a song or anything meant to be performed. It was simply a cry from my heart to hers. A scream lost in oblivion. My internal pain feels as sharp as if someone were trying to brand me with a hot iron, always pressing down on my heart and mind, and no matter how many times I plead for them to stop, the pressure increases, and I shrink away.

Yet, I know that no matter what room I am in or how many crowds I get lost in, I will always look for her. Could Dax say the same thing?

Throughout the upcoming week, my mood remains very stoic toward everything and everyone. I am easily irritated, and my grumpy attitude follows me wherever I go. Elena and I don't speak, and no matter how many times I look at her, she looks away as if talking to me would be wrong, like a betrayal.

Nights are spent hiding in my room when I'm not at work or band practice. I keep my blinds closed because I refuse to be tempted to check if Dax's car is parked outside or if the light is on in Elena's bedroom.

Come Friday morning, I stand under the shower faucet, feeling the warm water fall and cascade down my body, washing away whatever it can. Once I'm done, I step out and wrap a towel around myself, making my way toward the bathroom mirror, which is covered in fog.

Frank stands outside the bathroom, waiting to go in. He holds a coffee mug, and his tie is wrapped around his neck like a scarf. "Hey, kiddo. How's it going?"

"I feel like everyone asks me that all the time," I groan. "Is there anything else you want to ask?"

"We all care," he says, placing his free hand on my shoulder. "Your truck is all finished, by the way. They brought it over last night. Good as new."

I quickly get dressed and head outside to take a look. It does look good, almost new. It's an improved version from before. I want to see myself the same way.

When I'm ready to drive to school, I do so quietly. I don't even turn on the car radio. My mind feels overwhelmed, and I know I need to give it some space. As much as I would like to put on some music and get lost in someone else's feelings, I don't. I immerse myself in an unfamiliar silence that, strangely, becomes the perfect way to relax my nerves as I drive. I've decided to focus on what I can control. I will apologize to Stephanie. I will work on rebuilding my friendships and dedicate all my time and energy to the band.

After I pull into the student parking lot, I see Dax and Elena walking toward the building. Whatever they are talking about has Dax using theatrical hand gestures. It's only after Monty comes up from behind me, jumping on my back, that I realize why.

"Dude! Are you freaking pumped?!" he exclaims as his backpack drops to the pavement. I'm trying to process what the hell has him so excited, but I'm completely dumbfounded. "Wait—" he looks at me— "You don't know, do you? Didn't you listen to your answering machine this morning? I called like six times!"

"I can drive back home and listen to the messages now, or you could just tell me." I nudge him on the shoulder.

"Dude, we're going on tour! We'll be opening for a few other bands! Darryl had the label postpone our departure date until after graduation, but we'll start some shows locally, and then we're off like our caps and gowns!"

"Are you serious?" I said, grabbing him by both shoulders.

"Yep! And we get a tour bus and everything. We made it! We honestly made it!"

Before I realized it, we were jumping up and down like we were inside a moon bounce. This is the best news ever. We are on our way to becoming something big. It's one thing to be talented, and another to be signed. And it's an even bigger deal when a record label wants to invest in you. I always thought there was a "slight chance" we would make it, but I was wrong. The very thought makes me wonder if I've been wrong about other things? Maybe there was more to Dax and Elena than I refused to see?

Monty and I high-five before he darts after Dax. He leaps into his arms, continuing the celebration.

As for me, I lean back against my truck door, the same door that took most of the impact in the accident.

My parents showed me pictures of the wreck, but besides the rainstorm and being told it was one of the biggest storms to ever hit the area, everything else was a blur.

"As long as you don't have another head injury, you will be fine," the doctor tells me.

My parents seemed relieved. I was indifferent.

I crane my neck and watch the guys and Elena hugging each other. Even though I am just as ecstatic as they are, I can't bring myself to celebrate anything while she's there.

But what about a heart injury?

Chapter Twenty-Four
1998-1999

I'm sitting on my bed, fumbling with my journal. I open and close it, then open and close it again. My mind is having a hard time focusing, and I'm starting to wonder if I'll ever write anything again.

I finally opened it to the last page I had left off. I reread the words and try to work from there, but I'm struggling. I realize that so much of my heart has been yanked out of my chest and splattered into this journal that I doubt I have anything left to give.

Everything about my former self (Luke 1.0) was different. He wrote so much, so fearlessly. I only wish he could have carried that fearlessness into other areas of his life. If he had no fear, he would have gone after her. He would have fought harder. I wish I had been given the chance to fight again. Instead, I have no choice but to live vicariously through the pages of my past confessions.

My journal stays open, just like my heart, which is still sadly vulnerable. The emotions I've hidden begin to resurface. I wish I could forget how I feel. Suddenly, drops of water cause the ink to bleed as tears unexpectedly fall from my eyes.

It comes with a flash of lightning—or maybe I was confusing it with the rainstorm outside. I don't want to risk losing this momentum. I feel a new sense of purpose. A breath of fresh air has been breathed into me. I feel like a new man. Luke 2.0? Maybe that's what love does to you; it changes who you are—for the better.

My fate is undeniably connected to Elena. I may be young—perhaps immature to some—but my soul has always been mature.

Wilson is beside me, looking at me with those big puppy eyes. "I have to fight for her, don't I, boy?" He puts his head on my lap. "I think I need to talk to Dax first this time. It's only right."

I run toward my truck, nearly slipping a few times in the rain. Luckily, I catch myself before I fall because the last thing I need is another head injury. A part of me hesitates before I turn the key in the ignition. Did I feel comfortable driving in these conditions?

I toss my bag into the backseat and fasten my seatbelt. Through the rain pouring down on my truck, I suddenly see Elena on her porch. Her back is to me, and she is not alone.

As the months have gone by, I find myself further from Elena than I was before. I need to be honest and open with everyone. Not even this rain can hide me from her. I would drive through that storm again if it meant I was heading to her.

However, I don't start my truck. Instead, I watch Elena and Dax on her porch. I doubt they saw me run to my truck. Instead, I watch them, trying my best to figure out what they are doing. Soon, Dax gets up from his seat and paces the porch a few times with his hands behind his head. That's how I know something's wrong. He only looks like that when he's worried. Elena stays seated, unmoving.

He drops his hands and raises them into the air as if he's surrendering. His mouth moves, but I can't make out what he's saying. Elena then stands up and pushes her chair back. She's shouting, but all I can hear is the sound of rain pounding against my windows.

When Dax rushes off the porch, Elena turns and looks my way. Does she see me? I doubt it, given all the rain. The more I keep staring at her, the more I wonder if that's rain on her face or tears.

The last thing we need is more rain, and now I understand the meaning behind *No Rain* by Blind Melon.

Whatever happened between Elena and Dax hurts deep inside me. She rocks back and forth on her heels, looking toward the direction of my truck and then back at her house. She's crying. It's not because of the rain. She wipes her face before storming down her front porch steps into the pouring rain. Her parents' car is parked in the driveway, where she quickly retreats.

The engine roars to life, and I almost feel like my head's going to spin off my shoulders as I watch this. Where is she headed?

Without hesitation, I step out of my truck and walk over to her. I wave my arms in the air just before she begins pulling out of the driveway.

"Where are you going?!" I yell through the rain.

She rolls down the window, drenched from her tears and the rain.

She shouts back at me, "I've made a mess of everything!"

"Get out of the car! You are not going anywhere in this weather."

Whatever is happening, it begins to slice through my soul like a dagger I'm powerless to defend against. It feeds on my denial. It laughs in my face as I'm desperate to make whatever is causing her pain go away. It creates this urge within me that I cannot turn away from. I feel the adrenaline run through my veins until I'm certain I could tear off the car door and pull her out like some superhero. The more she cries, the more I crumble. Lately, my life seems to hang in an unstable balance. Nothing feels secure. Only she can ground me. I am begging to be grounded.

"Where do you think you're going?" I ask, holding the door open as the rain keeps falling harder, and all the remaining leaves from the trees are now scattered everywhere.

She rests her head on the steering wheel. "I don't know," she whimpers. "Dax thought you were working today. I was going to go down to the mall."

"I'm not working today. Either way, you shouldn't be driving in this. Plus, my truck is right here," I point.

"He convinced me that you didn't remember anything. He told me that if I tried to pursue things with you, you would just fake it. So, I panicked. I didn't know what to do."

"He said that?" I ask, pulling back slightly and gripping the edge of the door as the world starts spinning around me.

"He also told me that you loved her, not me." She wipes her eyes. "When I came that day to the hospital, he said that you woke up realizing you loved Stephanie, not me. Then, he told me he loved me," she says as my world comes to a screeching halt.

I stare back at her, wiping the rain from my eyes. But for the first time in a while, I see clearly. I reach out for her hand and hold it in mine as the familiar goosebumps return to their proper places. My heart begins to flutter, as if it has sprung back to life.

I gently pull her out of the vehicle and hold her in my arms as her body presses against mine. I don't know how long we can stay like this in the pouring rain, but I honestly don't care as long as she remains in my arms.

For so long, my feelings for her filled the gap that kept us from being honest with each other, which only grew stronger whenever we were in the same room. It was like trying to navigate through a field of emotional landmines while dodging unexpected grenades.

Just like a memory from long ago, I lift her chin and press her lips to mine. I kiss her, letting her know that I never stopped thinking about her— that I haven't stopped loving her. Tears flood our eyes, which we both pretend are still the rain. I can no longer hold back; I can no longer deny how much this girl means to me. Whatever happens is meant to happen, and I am so angry with myself for letting this go on for so long.

Even with all the uncertainty swirling in the air among the falling leaves and rain, we don't pull away. We draw ourselves closer. I understand in a way that I am making the same mistake twice, but when you want something badly (or love someone madly), you will do whatever it takes to get it.

"I've missed you," I breathe into the nape of her neck. I can taste the rain on her skin.

"I love you," she breathes back.

I pull away from her to get a good look at her. "You do?"

She nods, her hair dripping wet all over her face. I pull her close again, pressing harder as if I'm trying to penetrate souls. But there's something about how this embrace lingers and my refusal to let go that quickly makes me abandon all fear.

"Come with me," I say, leading her toward my house.

"Are your parents home?" she asks.

I shook my head and smiled as I guided her toward my house.

We're soaking wet, dripping water all over the foyer, forming large puddles on the floor; someone could drown in them. She shivers slightly just before pulling her shirt over her head and standing in front of me. Her bare skin is exposed, showing tiny goosebumps I now believe are contagious.

Again, I go to her. I lean down, resting my head against her shoulder. The movement surprises me, since all I want to do is keep staring at her. I pull myself back up and brush the hair that has fallen over her eyes. Water droplets slide down her face as I hold my hand to her cheek. Our eyes stay locked on each other. Neither of us seems to blink. I look at her cherry red lips. I watch as she moves them closer to mine. I notice her finger tracing along the lacy strap of her bra. I begin my lips' journey down to meet hers, and when they connect, I can taste the sweetness of her mouth again. I cannot pull away. She is a drug, and I'm too addicted, needing another fix from our last kiss.

Magnetized to each other, neither of us can seem to get enough as our mouths keep connecting without any desire to come up for air. The inside of my mouth feels her tongue's gentle touch, making my heart race so fast I fear it might explode. I fucking welcome it.

She awakens this unfamiliar animal instinct within me.

I lift her up until her legs straddle my body as I carry her up to my bedroom. I can't figure out how to keep moving without falling because I don't want to unlock my lips from hers.

I set her body down upon my bed until she is lying underneath me, arching her body as if trying to levitate. I lean into, smelling her scent as I reach my hand underneath her, cradling her body with every move that we make. Soon, the connection between our lips is broken as I tear off my shirt. She runs her fingers down my abs as I feel her nails run along the ridges like waves. I allow her to explore as much as she wants to, because when she is done, it will be my turn.

Rolling wages of electricity move through me as my body starts to lose control, as her fingers teasingly run along the waistband of my jeans. With one hand, she unbuckles my belt and slides down the zipper.

Her exploration continues until she takes me in her hand, and I groan into her open mouth. I slide my hand down her upper back until it unhooks her bra. I let my fingers linger until I end up tearing it off, which causes my eyes and hands to compete with one another on who gets to devour her first. But as soon as I announce the winner, she pushes my hand and slides it into her jeans.

She pulls me closer until the only thing between us is the movement of our hands. Our breaths are heavy, but we dare not stop for even a second. In the dim light, I look at her. She is truly beautiful. She is mine.

We don't say a single word to each other, and for some reason, I find comfort in that. There wouldn't be words to describe this moment even if I tried. So, I don't waste any time trying. I bite my lip as I open her up with my fingers and make my way inside. I try hard to focus my mind elsewhere, but her strokes intensify until I think I am going to burst before I get the chance to do anything more.

The anticipation is killing me. It's the most enjoyable slow death anyone could endure.

She leans in and presses her lips to my ear, and my eyes close at her touch. "I want you," she whispers.

"I want you," I whisper back. "Always have."

Her eyes stay fixed on me as a strand of hair falls over her face once again. This time, I leave it. I pull her in for another kiss, gently exploring the inside of her mouth with my tongue. All her clothing is gone. I'm surprised I didn't rip it off trying to get to her. I wonder if I ever want to be separated by such simple fabric again.

Our bare bodies are pressing harder against each other as my tongue takes leave and journeys onto her cheek, ear, and down her neck. Not stopping there, I let it run wild between her breasts, taking each perky nipple in my mouth. She moans my name. I could die.

I want nothing more than to experience what it's like inside her. Does she want that, too? As if reading my mind, her legs part wide open, giving me room to position my body as needed. Her lips tighten and then suddenly part, releasing sounds I never knew she could make—or that I could make her produce. I do the same. I could scream. The animal within me is begging to break free.

The blood rushes below my waist as I enter her. She cries out in pleasure as my thrusting intensifies. I kiss her lips as she yells out my name once more, our bodies instantly experience a sweet release that has been bottled up for too long.

I fall lifeless onto the bed next to her, trying to catch my breath. She rolls over and kisses me on the cheek.

"If you haven't guessed, I love you, too," I say.

And just like that, I realized that tricks aren't needed when the magic is real.

My journal is on my bedside table. Elena picks it up and says that every song I have written illustrates our story. Each one is like a chapter in our book. That's when she tells me she's serious about becoming a writer—to be the next R.L. Stine. She says she still uses the bookmark I bought her.

I watch her keep reading, but I don't stop her. I stay under my covers, holding her gently. When her eyes widen or linger longer on the page, I think she's trying to burn what I wrote into her memory. When she reads her favorite lines aloud, they sound like beautiful poetry.

I want to ask her what she is thinking when her lips curl into a smile. *Ugh, those lips. Those soft, lustful, supple lips. I can still feel how they found their way upon my body, branding me for life. An invisible tattoo that would cover me in ink if it were real.*

"Luke, you are an incredible writer," she says, "And I'm not just saying that because these are written all about me." She smirks.

"Do you really think so?"

We eventually talk about other things for a while. We talk about everything and nothing at the same time. We put in *Dumb and Dumber* and lie under the covers, refusing to return to our daily lives.

I reach over, pulling her closer. She turns and kisses me, her tongue softly sliding between my lips until they part, inviting her in.

For some reason, I find myself asking her what happened with Dax as she relaxes back into the crook of my arm.

"He told me the truth," she sighs. "That he lied about everything because he wanted to get back at you."

The weeks pass quickly. Fall gives way to winter, which then transitions into spring, and eventually spring gives way to summer. It's a continuous flow of moments that I have to quickly snap pictures of just to remember they happen. I can't count how many films from my camera I've had developed in such a short time.

My relationship with Elena has only grown stronger. Like a montage of moments, our connection also moves from one mixtape to the next. Countless hours spent waiting for the right song to play on the radio so I could hit the record button. I can hardly contain my happiness, with a permanent smile on my face that nothing in this world could destroy.

Dax and I finally cleared the air. It was long overdue, apparently. Since he had some things he wanted to get off his chest, just as much as I did. We're better now, even with Elena and me officially dating. I'm grateful that my friendship with him wasn't ruined, nor was the future of our band.

Elena and I pass notes all day at school, full of cheesy, sweet messages, describing how much we miss each other. We also started making each other mixtapes full of music that describes how we feel. It feels so good to be wanted. And it feels even better to be loved by someone as well.

Regarding the band, we have three gigs scheduled before we prepare for our small East Coast tour, where we'll be opening for a few well-known bands. On weekends, we spend our time in New York City working in the label's satellite studio, getting ready to release a few singles. They expect our first album to be out in May, before the tour begins. It's all too surreal to think about.

Even Darryl hired a temporary replacement at the store and extra summer help when we hit the road. However, as our departure date approaches, my excitement turns to sadness. I will be leaving Elena.

"You guys! You guys!" Dax bursts through the lunchroom doors with a small boombox in his hands.

"Where the hell did you get that?" Jordan points at the boombox just as Dax plops down at the table to join us.

"You guys, we are on the fucking radio!" Dax yells, silencing the tables around us.

He turns up the volume, and sure enough, his voice comes through the speakers. Our first single, *Pivot*, is playing for the world to hear or, at least, anyone tuned into the station and our school lunchroom.

Our song plays as Dax's voice echoes off the walls and surrounding tables, and I lose track of where I am—the feeling is transcendental. He sounds amazing. I can even hear my voice in the background. When it's over, everyone in the lunchroom erupts in cheers, and I can't help but grab my best friend and tell him how proud I am of him.

"If it weren't for your crazy idea, this would never have happened!" I exclaimed, hugging him.

"Snowball's chance, right?" he laughs, hugging me back.

"Maybe a slight chance." I wink.

Chapter Twenty-Five
1999

I take Wilson outside into the early morning sun. It shines from behind a transparent white cloud, which quickly passes overhead. The morning is already shaping up to be a very warm day, but luckily, a small breeze sweeps through as I watch the trees in my front yard sway.

Wilson runs toward the small red ball I toss. He grabs it with his mouth, then drops it on the ground by my feet. "You ready, boy?" I ask as I pick up the red ball. I fake a throw, and he turns to look, but he doesn't fall for it. I do this a few more times before I finally throw the ball for real.

We stay outside for a while when Elena walks out her front door to meet us. She takes turns throwing the ball to Wilson.

"I've always wanted a dog," she says after Wilson sprints toward the ball. "But my parents never caved in on that one. You would think they would have, considering I was their only child."

"Well, you can keep Wilson company while I'm gone. I'm sure he would love it," I offer.

"Did I ever tell you that I wanted a library? When I grow up, I want to build a house with a huge library and the comfiest chair for me to snuggle up and read." She smiles.

"Well, when you and I build our first house, I will make sure you get your library," I say just as Wilson goes after the ball again.

"I think I'm going to go to school for writing," she begins again. "After reading your words and given how much I love to read, it only makes sense. Don't you think? I want to write books that someone is obsessed with, like you and I are over Goosebumps," she chuckles.

"We are die-hard fans," I say.

"Like I-would-name-my-firstborn-after- R.L. Stine-fan," she chuckles louder.

"I will come to all of your signings," I say. "And I will always buy the first book, but it better be signed!"

"Are you saying we will be each other's number one fans?" she smirks.

"Babe, we already are."

The following Monday, I pull out of my driveway, ready for a long day at Record City, but I refuse to stop working until we go on tour. Or maybe it's because Darryl ordered us not to.

The store is playing our new music on repeat. The heavy wooden accents contrast with the neon glow of the lights that

Darryl installed for better musical aesthetics. We constantly flip through the poster display, imagining how it would feel to see our band picture in there. Or how cool would it be to hang on someone's bedroom wall?

However, instead of walking right in, I take a detour to the bookstore. Since we will be leaving on tour in less than a month, I wanted to pick up a couple of books to read during my downtime. I also thought it would be a nice idea to buy some for Elena to help pass the time.

I spent nearly my entire Record City paycheck at the store, hauling out three bags full of paperbacks. I wonder if they'll come up with a way to store books on a handheld computer one day. But then again, I think I'd always prefer the smell and feel of a book in my hands, no matter what inventions the future brings.

I sit by the fountain, counting my remaining change when I find the one penny among the other coins. So, what better way to spend it than to toss it into the fountain? Making a wish seems perfect.

As I close my eyes and throw it into the water, a hand gently presses on my shoulder. I open my eyes to see it's Elena.

Jeez, that was quick!" I glance at her and then at the fountain in disbelief.

"What do you mean? Were you expecting me?" she asks, as she sits down beside me.

"No, but I did wish for you, though." I smile.

"Why would you do that? You already have me." She kisses my cheek.

No matter how good Elena makes me feel, it still doesn't ease the ache I feel knowing I will be leaving her all summer. She tells me she has been accepted to a SUNY college in the fall, while I decide (against my parents' better judgment) to take a gap year. I really want to see how this band thing works out. Other than that, she and I haven't really talked about our future plans, which makes me think we're starting to live in a bubble that could burst at any moment.

"What's all this?" she asks, motioning to the bags.

"Well, you little sneak, it's a surprise," I say while trying my best to hide the bags.

"For me?" she beams. "Come on, let me take a peek." She reaches for one of the bags.

"You will just have to wait and see," I say as I reach over and pull her in for a hug.

She takes my hand in hers, caressing the top as she runs her thumb up and down the length of my palm. Once upon a time, I never understood what people meant by having their breath taken away by someone until I met her. Now it's as if my lungs have forgotten how to work. I stare down at our clasped hands—palm to palm, fingers entwined. A large piece of my puzzle has returned to me after being lost for some time. I hold her hand a little tighter, as if to show her I will never let her go. I could probably hold her hand like this forever. In this moment: a pile of books and a fountain full of wishes.

Hours fade away. Days disappear like morning dew. Weeks turn to dust beneath the relentless sun. The time has finally arrived for us to graduate, and then it's tour time.

Graduation day turned out just as I expected: eventful. We listened to enough speeches that I had to keep pinching myself so I wouldn't fall asleep. Once we were able to throw our caps in the air, I knew that this was truly the start of a new chapter in our lives. What was once our deadline turned into the beginning of what I hoped would be a long musical career.

Stephanie spots me in the crowd and approaches to wish me good luck. She hugs me and reassures me that there are no hard feelings.

"Yeah, good luck, man," Chase says as he comes up from behind her. "Sorry for being such a dick to you."

"Don't worry about it," I say, spotting Elena waiting for me in the distance.

"We are both going to the same college," Stephanie begins as if she needs to explain why the two of them are back together again. But I don't need an explanation. She owes me nothing. If anything, I owe her. She needs to know that I'm sorry and that I only wish the best for her.

So, I tell her.

I also shake Chase's hand before I make my way through the crowd of my former classmates toward Elena.

After we disrobe and hang up our caps, I close my eyes as the world spins around me. I grip tightly to my bedpost to try to ground myself, but it does little to help. The thought of leaving her feels like I'm losing her again. Still, I can't ask her to come. She needs to live her own life and follow her own path. I can't expect her to give up her dreams for mine.

She walks into my room and sits down beside me. We both knew this day was coming, but it doesn't make things any easier. It just tainted the days we had with sadness and fear.

She holds my hand and moves closer to me. My head instantly finds its place on her shoulder. I can feel her breathing. I inhale her scent: Sun-Ripened Raspberry by. I stare down at our hands, knowing that for a while, we won't have the luxury of simple things like these. The uncertainty of where our relationship will stand when I return scares me. Anything could happen. And no amount of reassurance from her eases that fear. There is no crystal ball for either of us.

"There is something I need to tell you," she begins. "And I don't want you to think that what happened between us in the past will ever happen again."

"What do you mean?" I ask.

"What I'm trying to say is, I never want to lose you again, Luke. The thought of losing you again hurts in parts of my soul I never knew existed," she explains.

I may be a former jock and now an aspiring rockstar, but this girl softens me to my core. The tears come without warning, and because she allows me to be one hundred percent authentic, I don't have to hide them. She wipes them away and kisses my cheek where they had fallen. Having once admitted that I never knew what love was before, I've decided that maybe love isn't so much about one big definition. Maybe, instead, it's made up of hundreds of little, undefinable things that mean much more.

"You know what I think?" I finally say to her. "I think what we have is fated."

"Like fated mates? That is my favorite trope!" she exclaims.

"What's a trope?"

"Never mind," she chuckles.

"Anyway, I know that when two people fall in love, there are always obstacles. Ours might be tougher than most at this age." I smile. "Even though I hate the thought of leaving you, and obviously I fear the worst, I have to believe we will be just fine," I say.

She cups my face in her hands and says, "We will be just fine."

"I love you so much, Elena Madison." I nestle my face deeper into the nape of her neck.

"And I love you, too, Luke Grant."

Later that night, as my mind drifts off to sleep, it forgets about the tangible present and gets lost in a kiss, a soft placement of her hand into my own, bodies intertwined, salt and sweat dropping like melting icicles. Suddenly, my eyes burst open without warning, and I instantly fly out of bed. I look inside my backpack and realize that something is missing.

My leather journal.

Where the hell is it?

It's midnight, and I'm tearing my room apart. Where the hell did I leave it? I retrace my steps in my mind as best as I can. The last time I had it was at practice, right? Did I leave it at Dax's by mistake? I can't imagine him opening it up to see that I'm still writing about his girlfriend.

Wait. I rub the sleep out of my eyes. *What am I even talking about?* I quickly realized it was all just a dream. There is nothing left to hide.

I'm having trouble falling back asleep, so I grab a flashlight from my closet and shine it into Elena's bedroom. I do this several times until she appears in the window. She waves her hand but quickly pulls it back to her face as she yawns.

I shine the flashlight down into the yard, signaling her to come over. She nods like she understands, and before I realize it, I'm outside under the stars, waiting for her.

We lie in the grass, gazing up at the clear night sky. The stars shine brightly, and we spend some time guessing the constellations. I am not very good at this, so I make up my own.

"That doesn't exist," she laughs.

"Now, now. I did point out the Big Dipper," I counter.

"A toddler could have picked out the Big Dipper," she laughs again.

"I wish we could stay like this forever," I say.

"Come winter, we will freeze to death," she replies. "How about we just enjoy this moment now?"

"Sounds perfect to me." I wink.

"Oh, really? You look like you've got something up your sleeve," she says.

I place my finger to my lips before leaning over and pressing them against hers. "Try to be quiet," I whisper.

"What do you mean?" she whispers back as I start to pull down her pajama bottoms, followed by her pink thong.

My fingers find their way inside of her as she quietly moans into the night. Then, as my face goes in between her legs, my tongue forces her to rip the grass from the roots to stifle what I know was meant to be a scream.

Chapter Twenty-Six
Now

We have two hours left of our drive. It might as well be an eternity.

"Wait, so is this the same truck you got into your accident with?" Robbie asks, running his hand along the dash.

"The very one," I say. "I actually ended up liking it a lot more after it was fixed up." I tap the steering wheel.

"Do you still have trouble remembering things?" he asks, the question I knew he was bound to eventually ask. *Isn't it the very reason I'm in this mess?*

"Listen, kid." Monty leans forward with a small bag of chips in his hand. "It's more complicated than you think."

"Put your seatbelt back on," I cut in.

He leans back, buckling himself in. "Anyway, I'm only going to say this because Luke and I have been friends for decades, but love makes you tread some dangerous waters on a good day.

Imagine treading those waters when you have no idea if land is in sight."

Small beads of sweat form on my forehead, so I grab an extra napkin to blot them away. The more I've gotten to know Robbie, the more I rediscover parts of myself I had no reason to search for. Maybe I've been approaching this whole journey the wrong way?

"But he seemed fine after a while," he responds to Monty as though I am no longer in the truck. "How could he go backwards? I don't understand. I feel like there is so much I'm not understanding." His face is full of wonder and concern.

Against my better judgment, I glance in the rearview mirror at Monty. I know he's aware. He's just holding back for reasons I still don't fully understand. I've tested the waters enough. Just dunk me in already.

"But you got together. None of this is making sense," Robbie continues. "I take it you broke up while you went on tour? But that doesn't make sense either."

"Our paths were synchronized with each other for a long time. When I moved, she moved and vice versa. Yet, that synchronization made it harder as my music career took off. But I didn't give up, if that is what you are asking," I say.

"Then what happened? Why don't you remember?" His head snaps toward me.

"I didn't just jump ship, kid. Neither did she. But sometimes in life, when you don't know which way is right, you retreat. It's natural," I try to explain.

"But that's not true, Luke. You know that, right?" Monty cuts in from the back.

It's not?

I've been asked this very question several times before. I can't even count how many times I've asked myself. My eyes fall to my watch, which I twist slightly on my wrist. The time seems to slow down, and my anxiety quickens. I watch as the second hand continues ticking away as if it has no awareness of how I feel. Is this trip pointless? Should I turn back? They say you can always go home again, but can you always go back to the '90s?

I roll down the window slightly as the outside air circulates inside the truck. I imagine being transported back to that time. The heavy wooden accents. The absence of modern technology. The ability to work for genuine connections instead of the false sense of achievement from becoming someone's "friend" with a single click.

The smells. The food. The feeling that nothing was dangerous and the day only ended when the streetlights came on. You were found where you left your bike or skateboard.

TV wasn't on demand. Mixtapes took effort. You had to have your boombox ready to record after the radio DJ announced the song. They were personalized—decorated with black marker with names to show the meaning behind the mix.

I could get lost in that time. It pulls me back there as if it's kept just for me to visit whenever nostalgia hits.

Robbie is still staring at me, waiting for an answer as a wave of emotion crashes over me, almost knocking me down.

I see Elena. Her face is expressionless, just like mine. I watch as my hand reaches out to her for forgiveness, but I can't tell if she reaches back. Soon, she fades into a ghostly silhouette and disappears from view.

My eyes blur at the sudden appearance and disappearance of her. I blink, then refocus. But I see nothing but the roaring crowd. The stage looks like an infinity pool, and for some reason, I find myself inching closer and closer to the edge. The guys are in their element. We all are. We're only focused on hitting the right notes and pumping up the crowd.

My guitar is on me, but I can barely feel it in my hands. I'm only feeling the music as I practically levitate. The cheering from the crowd begins to grow louder, pulling me closer and closer.

As I turn back, I hear Jordan yell something from the corner of the stage, but I can barely make out the words. He points to something behind me, which I think is his way of saying that the crowd loves us. I nod at him because I know they do.

Yet, he keeps pointing repeatedly with growing frustration. Monty soon understands, and I immediately find myself caught in the babble of an incoherent conversation.

I step back, and suddenly I lose my footing. I fall from the stage into the crowd below. My guitar crashes against the floor, along with my head. I can barely breathe as the audience begins swarming me like bees. It's getting dark. I can barely see any light, no matter how hard I try to find my way out of the crowd. Then, I hear nothing as if everything is inside a vacuum, and then I'm back in a very familiar darkness.

"Dude, you're sweating," Monty says from the backseat. "Are you OK? You don't look it. Maybe I should drive?"

I take a sip of my bottled water. "I'll be fine. Just give me a minute.

"Seriously, I think I should drive. And I'm not taking no for an answer, Luke."

But before I say anything to him, I notice Robbie has his phone pressed against his ear. A somber expression takes over his face.

"Who did you call?" I ask.

He sighs. "I will tell you, but you have to answer one thing for me first."

"What's that?" I ask.

"Do you remember me?

Chapter Twenty-Seven
1999

We're off.

"Are you OK?" Elena asks as I pack up my luggage. Three months of touring felt much shorter before she was in the picture. Now it suddenly seems like I'll be gone forever. I know she feels the same way, which makes this all still seem like a dream I'm about to wake up from.

I set my bag down and go to her, wrapping my arms around her tightly. It feels as if I'm scared she'll fly away if I let go.

"I'm proud of you. Do you know that?" She looks up at me.

"It means more to me than you'd ever know." I nuzzle my face into her shoulder. I breathe in her perfume, which may be a popular scent, but it only makes me think of her.

"Ugh, I don't want to go," I say, fighting back tears that are begging to burst from my eyes.

"You have to," she says to me. "You would regret it if you never took this chance. You all would," she replies.

"What about you?" I ask as I hear the muffled sounds of my bandmates from downstairs. I do my best to ignore their excited cheers and laughter as they start pumping themselves up for what they think will be a life-changing, epic journey. Who would have guessed that our small high school band would get this far? It's still shocking that we were signed to a label and about to release our debut album.

"I'll be fine. Wilson will keep me company." She pats him on the head when he comes and sits at her feet. "Oh, and try to keep Dax in line. He seems like he might need some hand-holding," she teases. "I don't want to have to bail you idiots out of jail."

Once the muffled voices have mostly stopped, I pull away from her and bend down to pick up my bags.

"Do you have everything?" she asks.

I tilt my head at her. "Not everything."

She smiles at this because deep down, she knows this goodbye is much harder than either of us wants to admit. There is so much left unsaid. It's a melody that touches the heart more than those three little words ever could.

Still, those three little words are held in the air with a definite period—a statement, a truth, firm and unwavering, and permanent. Somewhere between us falling out of love, the words have kept spilling from my lips, making up for every moment I couldn't say them out loud.

We walk out of my bedroom, standing far enough apart to commit our images to memory. I linger, holding onto the goodbye, afraid to let it go.

However, it was at that moment that I realized no matter how much I loved this girl, it was no good to hold her back from her dreams and ask her to come along. If we are meant to be together, if we were truly "fated mates" as she put it, we would get through this. Three months versus a lifetime was nothing in the grand scheme of things. I had suffered long enough when I didn't have her, so I knew that to keep things going, we would have to work at it. She was the reason for every note I played on my guitar and every word I had written into song. With her, I have found rhythm. I have found balance. Most of all, I have found purpose. It was the art of holding on.

I do my best to fake a smile, ignoring my screaming heart. *Oh, how it begged me to just let it all out—to tell her how I really felt—to beg her to come*. Instead, I told her how proud I was of her, too. She was going to school and pursuing her dream of becoming a writer.

"Number one fans, right?" she says, looking at me. In her eyes, I see so much love—love I feel I have no choice but to walk away from.

I couldn't help but wonder what she saw in my eyes because all I could see in hers was my future wife.

We head down the stairs, where my stepdad Frank is talking with Dax.

Frank greets me as I walk down the stairwell, pulling me in for a hug — tighter than I ever remembered my real father giving. When we pull apart, he wears the biggest, proudest grin on his face.

"You guys all ready to go?" He looks around at us.

"Where's Monty?" I ask, noticing his absence.

"He's in the bathroom," Dax answers. "He'll be out once he's done powdering his nose."

"And how are you holding up, Miss Madison?" Frank asks Elena next.

I watch as her lip slightly trembles. She bites down on it to prevent herself from crying. "I'm good," she lies on my behalf.

"They will be home before you know it. One summer, and this could be the key to many of your futures. But just remember, you are not invincible. You need to be respectful and learn about this business as much as you can," he instructs.

"Thank you for saying that," Darryl cuts in. "They normally roll their eyes whenever I tell them anything."

"Please call me every day!" my mom bursts into the room, a dish towel draped over her shoulder.

"That goes for you, too, Mister." She pinches Dax on the cheek before pulling me into a hug. "I packed a cooler full of food for you boys while you're on the road. There is meatloaf, a pork loin, and several casseroles that you can heat up in the microwave. You do have a microwave in that giant camper of yours, right?"

"It's a tour bus, Mom. Of course, there's a microwave." I smile as my finger traces the small, ripped seam on my bag just as Frank takes the cooler from my mom and drags it outside.

"Dax, is there a fridge where you can store the food? I'd hate for you to have to keep replacing the ice when it melts," my mom calls out to him after he walks out of the house.

"It's a tour bus, Ms. G., of course, there's a fridge!"

I take a look at the tour bus, which looks like a mobile home on wheels, and I quickly begin to feel the excitement building toward this new chapter.

Then again, my chosen career was never music. At one point, I thought I would become a teacher or something similar, but after signing our contract and hearing about the tour, a part of me wondered if I had it all wrong. Of course, my parents worried that I would have nothing to fall back on if this music career didn't take off as we hoped, so I ended up promising them I would attend college if that happened.

After all our luggage and gear had been safely packed and stowed away, we started climbing into the bus to depart. Darryl was talking with the driver as they both held out a map, pointing to all the stops we had planned and places we wanted to visit along the way (if time allowed).

I hugged Elena one last time before climbing onto the tour bus.

"Good luck, boys!" She waves at us. "And behave!"

Then, just as the driver was seconds from pulling away from the curb, I realized I had forgotten to give Elena the books I bought her.

I knocked on the window to get her attention while yelling at the driver to stop the bus.

I run toward the door and yell her name while trying to catch my breath. "In my bedroom closet, there are three bags. I bought you a book to read for every week we are gone."

But before she could respond, the driver tells me to step back from the door. "We have to stay on schedule, Mr. Grant." He nods in my direction.

I make my way back to my seat, pressing my face firmly against the window, counting all the houses we pass. I pay close attention to the intricate details of the neighborhood. It's funny how things look different when you leave them behind.

Have we finally made it?
Considering I have Elena. Fuck yeah, I made it.

Chapter Twenty-Eight
1999

While on tour, I would count backwards from ten to one and imagine that when I reached one, she would appear. When she didn't, I'd feel disappointed—unless, of course, I conjured the perfect image of her in my mind. That would have to do for now. There really was no better way to stay connected.

I think of Elena at ten, the first time I knocked on her door when the Goosebumps books fell onto her driveway. The way she smiled at me at nine and how I instantly felt weak in the knees. Her lips pressed against mine at eight. And at seven, feeling the warmth of her breath against my skin as my hands explored her body. When she told me she loved me at six; and at five, when I told her how much I loved her, too. At four, when I was inside of her. Three, how she tastes. Two, when we realized we belonged together, and one, when I knew she was The One.

Slight Chance performed at ten different shows in ten different locations along the East Coast. At one show in Boston, Elena surprised me by flying down to attend the concert. In fairytales, the hero or prince is always depicted as the knight in shining armor, riding in on his white horse to rescue the damsel in distress or princess, but the story is rarely told from the opposite side. Sometimes, the prince needs saving too, and Elena has done that for me.

When September arrived, Elena headed to college. She emailed me a picture of our band's poster hanging on her dorm room wall. It felt very surreal. I also missed her a lot.

However, the tour was a success, along with the release of our debut album, so we extended the tour by another three months. The label then urged us to move to California to build our image and take advantage of the star power there. Everyone agreed—even Darryl—but I was hesitant.

"I'm so glad I'm not in a relationship," Dax huffed as he flopped onto the hotel bed. We had just landed in L.A. and didn't want to spend another night on the tour bus.

"It's not bad," I reply. "I just never imagined leaving like this."

"Well, if it's meant to be, you guys will be just fine," Monty says while looking inside the mini-fridge.

"I just need time to think about this whole move thing. Don't you guys think this is all just too much?" I sit down on the edge of the bed.

"Too much?" Dax sits up. "If you don't come, it ruins it for all of us. Don't be *that* guy."

So, I wasn't *that guy*.

Because we moved to California.

The guys made a good point that if I just left and went back to New York, I would end up sitting around while she was off doing her college thing. I agreed to work things out with Elena so that we could travel back and forth as much as possible.

Come November, she flew out to stay with us at our new beachfront apartment. It wasn't fancy, but it was pretty spacious, and it was ours. The view from the back porch to the beach was breathtaking, and I spent most of my time outside enjoying the scenery and writing new music.

One night, while the guys all went out. She and I stayed back for some alone time. Since we hadn't had much privacy, I wanted to take full advantage of our last night together—no restricted movements. No censored screams. I wanted to devour every inch of her, and I wanted to hear how much she liked it.

We are in the kitchen. I open a bottle of wine and pour each of us a glass.

"Fancy." She smiles. "Since when do you guys have wine glasses?"

"Came with the apartment." I clinked her glass with mine.

She hops onto the island and takes another sip of her wine. Her tiny yellow sundress barely covers much as she sits in front of me. I look up at her and step between her legs as she straddles me, pulling me in for a kiss.

"I've missed this," she moans into my ear.

"You have no idea," I say.

Gently, I ease her back until she is lying completely down. Her hair flows down the side of the island like an Auburn waterfall. I duck down and go to remove her panties, but to my surprise, she isn't wearing any.

"Well, Elena, this is a first," I say before sliding my tongue up and down her clit.

The week of her visit flew by too quickly. We didn't have enough time for everything we wanted or planned to do. And since I had to take her back to the airport, there was this lingering feeling of uncertainty between us that I couldn't quite grasp. Where did it come from? And why was it here?

When I finally parked, it all made sense: when will we see each other again?

"You can't promise me that," she says as we walk from the parking lot into the airport. "You can't promise me that everything will be fine because neither of us can see into the future."

"Yes, but Elena, you *are* my future," I reply.

"Luke, nothing in life is guaranteed. You are out here in California living your best life, and I'm happy for you, but I'm living my own back in New York. We aren't crossing paths the way we should. There is a reason why long-distance relationships never work out. It's hard," she says.

I reach for her hand. "It's not hard unless we make it hard."

"It's just words," she replies. "Because we both know that it's hard. No matter how you try to spin things, our situation sucks."

"I didn't know you felt that way." I retreat.

"I just feel like I'm going to lose you no matter how many times I fly out here to see you or you come home to see me," she begins to cry.

"Why would you ever think you would lose me?" I ask.

"Because," she says, "we are young. We have so much life ahead of us that sometimes I think it would be foolish to ignore that. If we are holding each other back, then that should be our dealbreaker."

"Do you think I'm holding you back?" I ask as a crowd of people rushes past us toward the ticket counter. All I can hear right now is the airport announcements and the pounding of my heartbeat.

"No, but I think I'm holding you back, and that worries me," she confesses.

"You are not holding me back," I set her bag down on the floor.

"Well, I feel like I am..." Her voice trails off and lifts with the rising planes.

"Listen, I know that I love you, and that means more to me than any uncertainty this world throws at us," I say.

Through tears begging for release, I force a reassuring smile onto my face as she walks toward the ticket counter. I'm not being foolish, am I? I know there are many reasons why long-distance relationships often fail. I wonder if ours will be any different.

Large swarms of people continue to buzz around us like bees as Elena and I try to figure out the best way to say our goodbyes.

"Please, don't cry," I say when I see her face start to redden. "It will go by fast. We will talk on the phone all the time. I will be better at AIM," I chuckle. "Then, it's my turn to come home."

She nods her head as she wipes tears from her eyes. "Ok," she says before giving me a final hug goodbye. And before I could say anything more, she slips away into the crowd and out of sight.

Admit
One
Three Years Later

Chapter Twenty-Nine
2002

What the hell? Is this really what the world is coming to? No, the world didn't end, nor did we revert to the Stone Age when the year 2000 arrived. Instead, we keep finding new ways to connect, which somehow seems to backfire. Am I the only one who thinks this? Honestly, I don't get this social media stuff. I tried it because Darryl wants us to stay cutting-edge, but I can't think of eight people I want to list as my top friends. And why the hell do I have to rank them?

For three years, Elena and I lived apart — she in New York and me in California. The band was gaining popularity, and the only time I made it out that way besides being home for Christmas was when we appeared on MTV's TRL in New York City. We literally stood above Times Square while a studio audience cheered us on for making one of the top-requested videos. We were on cloud nine (or the 36th floor of the MTV Studios building, same difference).

We even won an MTV Video Music Award, which nearly gave Dax and Jordan a heart attack. We were thriving. As for Monty, he was receiving a lot of praise for his drumming skills, while Dax was soaking in all the fame (he even ended up landing a girlfriend from America's Next Top Model). As for me, I focused on the music and Elena as much as I could. We were far from the naive kids who had fallen in love when the world told us love was easy. Now, we were facing various obstacles that neither of us had the tools to fight.

The media was relentless. They followed us around, capturing whatever pictures they could to support their false narratives. Several times, Elena would call me in a panic whenever she read something in a magazine. The latest gossip column falsely reported that I was dating some girl from the music scene. It was exhausting dealing with this stuff. And it was also exhausting having to reassure her repeatedly that none of what she was reading was true.

Either way, we started fighting. A lot.

"I want to know," she yells into the phone, "do you even love me? Because from what I see, it doesn't seem that way!"

"Elena, I have told you countless times not to pay attention to those gossip magazines. That is all they are — gossip. You should believe me," I say.

"I just don't know how we'll recover from this," she continues. "My parents and friends even started asking questions. It doesn't look good."

"Come back from what?" I ask, stepping onto the porch with my cell phone, away from the guys' earshot. The last thing I needed was for them to overhear us arguing for the hundredth time that week.

"All of this," she repeats. "How do we fix this?"

"Well, I guess I wasn't aware that we needed fixing," I say. "It's just not fair how you keep blaming me. You know I love you. You know I'm faithful to you, yet you keep acting like I don't believe or care about those things—like I'm not keeping my promises. I can't live in a bubble and expect our band to keep rising to fame. There's an image I'm supposed to maintain. And as much as I hate it, I have to go to events with the guys. I have to be seen by the paparazzi. But just because I shake a girl's hand or even hug someone, doesn't mean anything more than a polite gesture."

"I want to know, do you love me?" she asks, acting as if she hadn't heard a single word I said.

"Damn it, Elena!" I yell. "Of course, I fucking love you. If I didn't, I wouldn't be putting up with all of this shit."

"Oh, so you're putting up with me now, is that it?" she snaps.

"You know what I mean. Don't try to twist my words," I reply.

"Whatever, Luke. Just live your rockstar life and forget all about me. Even better, forget about me visiting next month as well," she continues.

"Are you serious? What the fuck, Elena? Are you breaking up with me or something?" I find myself pacing the back porch until I'm sure I'm carving wooden footprints into the planks.

"Maybe we should just take a break. You know, *pivot*, for a little while," she says.

Her words shot out of her mouth like bullets, piercing me to the core. I leaned over the porch railing, wanting either to jump off or out of my skin. I've come to realize that, over the years, relationships take a lot of work. You can sugarcoat it as much as you like, but the truth is the truth. Like with work, they say if you do something you love, you never work a day in your life. Well, when it comes to relationships, if you're with someone you love, it never feels like work. Elena has always been my passion.

"Honestly, I don't even know what the hell to say right now. Are you really throwing that song in my face?" I ask, but before I could even talk her out of this nonsense, she disconnected the call.

If a soul could cry, mine was definitely bawling its eyes out. I'm pretty sure that the heavens could feel it because a few drops of rain hit my forearm just as I went to brush away some tears. I don't care that I cry. And I certainly don't care if the guys or the world knows I do either. Crying isn't a weakness. It's the strength to allow yourself to be vulnerable and to stay true to your emotions instead of hiding them for other people's benefit.

I walk back into the house, where the guys are all gathered around the kitchen island, eating food and having drinks. I walk over to the fridge and reach for a beer. I want to shatter into a million pieces. Everything I once thought was solid in my life just crumbled before my very own eyes. And for what? Because some stupid magazine wrote about fake news?

I pull out my phone and stare at the picture I saved of us. Elena and I are laughing. It was a candid moment that showed more love than any staged picture ever could. I walk closer, taking a sip of my beer as the cold ale coats my throat. I look at her. I look at her smile. There's no way I'm giving up on this girl. It's under that realization (or maybe that determination) that I will do whatever I can to salvage this.

I have to salvage this.

What I didn't get was why her parents and friends were fueling her doubt. It's not like they knew what was real. They didn't understand me like she does. Didn't she tell them everything I said in hopes of calming her? There was really nothing left for me to do except put a ring on her finger.

Should I have asked her to marry me? Honestly, I would have asked her the first day I met her, but to be honest, I wanted her to finish school. I wanted her to land a job. I didn't want to make things difficult by making her feel like I was forcing her to choose between my life and hers. I thought I was doing the right thing. Apparently, I was not.

"You OK, man?" Jordan walks up beside me, looking down at the picture on my phone. He shaved his head recently, and I still find it hard not to laugh when I see him.

"We broke up," I say.

"I kind of figured that. I'm sorry." He puts his arm around me. In the fifteen years I've known him, this is the first time we've shared a moment like this. It's also the first time I've felt genuine friendship with him.

"Sorry about what?" Monty says as he steps up on my other side.

"They broke up," Jordan answers for me.

"Really? Fuck, man. That's rough. I'm sorry, too," Dax says from behind me.

We are literally in a huddle now, staring at my phone as if an answer to my problem is somewhere there.

"Not to be all sappy, but I read this book…" Monty begins just as Jordan's bald head whips in his direction.

"You read a book?" I close my phone.

"I know how to read, asshole." He smacks me in the back of the head. "Anyway, it was some fantasy book, but I got really into it. The point I'm trying to make is that the two main characters were constantly facing shit, but somehow they always found their way back to each other. It was like—"

"Fate?" I bite my lip. "Like fated mates?"

"Sure, whatever you want to call it," he says. "Well, it made me think of you two, which means you will find your way back to each other. I know it."

Months pass, and the sense of time quickly slips away. I'm outside on the back deck, feeling lost. Several times, I close my eyes and then force them open again, convinced that everything that happened was just a dream. But reality won't let the illusion last long.

Even from far across the country, I can feel her breathe. I can hear her heartbeat. I can smell her. I can feel her head rest against my chest as her arms wrap around me.

She will always have doubts, which is normal. But I never did. So, if I decide to do anything, I guess it's time to book a ticket and go back home.

With her, I can always go home again.

Chapter Thirty
2002

I'm home. Sitting in the backseat of a cab, I'm staring at my childhood home—and of course, hers. So much has changed, yet it all remains the same. It's a strange thing to explain. You have to experience it to fully understand.

I left before the new millennium began, believing I knew exactly who I was. I also left unaware of which version of myself would come back. I'm still trying to figure that out now.

"You all right, man?" the cab driver interrupts my thoughts.

"Yeah," I clear my throat. "Just trying to emotionally prepare myself."

"Don't worry. Take all the time you need," he offers before turning around in his seat. "Wait, you're that guy?"

"I'm *that* guy," I say as I grab my bag.

After I pay the driver and he drives away, I walk up the driveway, hoping that my parents are no longer foolish enough to hide the key under the mat. Sure enough, when I get to the front door, there it was.

I walk into my childhood home. The atmosphere feels different. It feels like home, but not quite. Again, it's hard to explain. You would have to experience it to understand fully. It looks exactly the way I left it. Yet, it feels strange. It's a preserved memory that my present self just doesn't fit into. I am the object out of place. So far removed from the 'once was,' searching for a place to still belong.

The house is empty, and the silence feels almost eerie. There is new furniture throughout, along with new artwork on the walls. But my bedroom is still stuck in 1999 and has never quite moved on. I think a part of me hasn't moved on either. The '90s have me in a chokehold, and I long to feel that way again. It's heartbreaking to realize I never will.

I walk slowly into my old room as if waiting for permission. Wilson barely lifts his head off my bed, where he still sleeps. His golden head is white, and it saddens me to think how much of his life I missed out on these past few years. I thought about taking him out to California, but I quickly realized it would not have been a good decision.

I lay down beside him, resting my head on the same pillow I used for most of my teenage years. It still bears a slight imprint. I end up closing my eyes, pretending Elena is lying next to me like she once did. However, I wake up an hour late with my mom standing in the doorway.

"She doesn't live next door anymore, you know?" she says, before coming to sit down beside me.

"I know. I'm just afraid," I admit. "I never imagined we'd reach this point. I thought we'd be the exception."

"*Except* that exceptions are never really what they seem. You have to accept what the rules are and adapt from there," she says.

"I swear I never did anything to hurt her. I never would," I say, as if she ever thought otherwise.

"Distance creates distance." She puts her arm around my shoulder as soon as I sit up next to her. "Whether you wanted it to or not, it's the nature of things."

"Yes, but I can't control what they write about me, Mom," I say.

"No, you can't. Nor can you control how other people feel about it either," she consoles.

"I started writing again—in my journal. I considered releasing it all. You know, as 'the grand gesture.'"

My mom smiles again. "Well, you've always had a way with words. I'm sure whatever you've written is beautiful."

"Where is she? Do you know?" I ask my mom.

"Mrs. Madison told me she rents an apartment about fifteen minutes from here. I can give you the address," she offers.

"Please," I say as she reaches for my phone and enters the address. "Do you mind if I borrow your car?" I ask her.

"Keys are on the counter."

"Thanks, Mom." I hugged her. "If I don't come back tonight, consider it a good sign."

My nerves grow more intense as I approach my destination. What if she has moved on? What if I knock on her door and she's with someone else? Still, buried beneath the doubts that suffocate me inside my mother's car, I picture us embracing like reunited lovers. It's a long shot. But if I've learned anything in life so far, it's that even the slightest of chances still count.

I arrived.

I'm here.

I pull into the driveway of a grey townhouse that honestly suits her. She has a wreath on the door and a small chair on the porch. Beside the chair is a pot of flowers, which I know is her reading spot. For a moment, I feel sadness from the reminder of how much she wanted a home library. If anything, I hope the inside is full of books. I've always wanted her to be happy, but I still wish I could be the reason for her happiness.

I walk up the porch steps and knock. I don't allow myself to hesitate because the moment I do, I will lose my courage. I have to accept that whatever happens, happens. I have to let fate take control.

A few seconds later, the door opens. She stands in a vibrant blue dress that highlights her figure perfectly.

Behind her, a candle is lit on a small table, casting flickering shadows across the white walls. Elena stands, arms crossed, watching me as if trying to decide whether I'm a mirage. The dress she is wearing ties at her waist and ends a few inches above her knees. Instantly, I'm transported to that time in California when she wore that yellow sundress with nothing underneath.

As much as I want to focus on what's hidden underneath, a necklace she wears catches my eye instead. It looks like the exact same flower is etched on the cover of my journal.

The silence between us is heavy but not cold. It feels weighed down by sadness, regret, and all the words we left unsaid. Two people in love shouldn't have to face this. Love should have the power to eradicate it.

I remain standing in the doorway, looking at her. My chest rises slowly under the weight of the moment pressing down on me. "Elena," I finally say, steadying myself with the doorframe. I fear my knees might give out.

"Luke," she says, fiddling with her necklace.

"Is that the same flower?" I ask.

"Yes," she says. "I had it made. It's you," her words scatter like mice, and I'm trying my best to catch them before they disappear. "It's always been you."

Instead of responding, I push off from the doorway with strength instantly returning to my knees. "It's always been you, too," I say as the time we lost folded like paper.

Pulling her in for a long-awaited embrace, my hand gently runs through her hair as I cradle her head to kiss her. But just like anything that tastes good, you can't just have one bite. You have to devour it. And that is what I plan to do—devour her.

A pause.

Our breathing now synchronized—a quiet rhythm aching with an old familiarity—our place of comfort—of home.

"I missed you so much," she whispers. "I'm sorry for everything. I was being foolish."

"No," I stop her. "I'm here. It's OK. *We* will be OK."

My hands find her waist and pull her even closer. Our lips meet again, slow and searching, like a promise. It's been a lifetime of laughter, nights in each other's arms, and the ache from pockets of time we lost.

My fingers trace along her jawline and the curve of her back as she runs her hand beneath my shirt, like she's rediscovering a favorite song—one made just for her. Words that only we know how to sing.

Clothes are torn off in haste. A pile of blue like the ocean pools at her feet. Each touch behaves like the reassurance we desperately needed.

For the entire night, we lay in a naked embrace on her bed. No sooner than we are making love, we find ourselves back at it again as if catching up on lost time, until our bodies cry out for nourishment. Luckily, her roommate wasn't home, so we entered the kitchen without clothes for something to drink.

Elena quickly chugs her glass of water as I wipe the beads of sweat off my chest with a paper towel. She sets her glass down on the counter and walks over to me, licking the remaining residue off my chest as if the water wasn't enough to quench her thirst. Slowly, she turns around until her ass is pressed up against me. Then, she bends over as I slide right in, her sweetness dripping all over me like honey.

"Come back to California," I say to her after.

"I can't, Luke. I need to finish school," she says.

"Transfer. Finish school in California. You want to be a writer; you can write anywhere!" I almost beg.

She hesitates as if considering my idea. We wouldn't have to do the long-distance song and dance anymore. She could stay with me all the time. We could start building our life together. But before I can even imagine a future with Elena in California, she says, "How about I come visit, and then we can decide?"

"Deal." I take her finger and cross it into mine.

Chapter Thirty-One
2002-2014

California here we come. Right back where we started from.

It was so different this time. Elena came to visit as she promised. She stayed for a few weeks while we figured out what it would be like if she lived here. I know I made enough money to support her while she finished school, so financially, I wasn't worried. My only concern was that she might end up resenting me. Resentment was the last thing I wanted. Sometimes, choices can lead to that, so I wanted her to make the best decision for herself and to know that no matter what she chose, I would always be there—nothing would change.

However, an internship unexpectedly came her way while we were lying in bed one morning. She checked her e-mail and instantly began to cheer. She had wanted to work for a publishing company for the longest time, and this summer, she would be interning at one. She applied for several years and was never selected. As luck would have it, she was chosen now.

"You have to go,' I say. There's no way I could stop her from doing this. "Where is it?"

"New York City. It's truly a dream," she beams. "I've been trying to get into this internship for years, but I was never chosen. I never understood why, but now it doesn't matter, because they picked me! I can't believe it." Her hand covers her mouth in shock. "I have to take it, right?" She looks at me for confirmation.

"Yes, you have to," I say. "You can't pass this up."

Knowing that the label had a studio in NYC, I wondered if I could leave California instead. However, I know the guys would never be OK with that, but I still mentioned it to them before I even brought it up to Elena.

"You're nuts," Jordan says to me, closing the fridge door. Elena was in the shower, and I knew we had a few minutes before she could hear us talking.

"We only have a few more shows out here, and we're not going to start working on another album for a few months. Why would it be nuts?" I counter.

"Because it just makes it look like we are not a united front. It gives the perception like we're breaking up," Dax cuts in.

"Unfortunately, I'm dealing with that on both ends." I shake my head. "It's not permanent, you know? I will be back."

"*Will* you?" Dax looks at me. "I know we have had our differences in the past, but I know you, Luke. You won't be back."

"Monty?" I turned to him. From the beginning of the conversation, he hasn't said a word.

"Honestly, if you leave, it may be the end of Slight Chance," he says.

"You're not serious?" I look at the guys. I was being given an awful decision. What would I pick? Better yet, *who* would I pick? How could I pick one over the other? And why did I even have to?

"You've always followed your heart," Monty says.

"Yeah, and your heart has always been with her—not us." Dax slouches in response to the weight of his words.

"That's not true. I love you guys," I say.

"We know," Jordan puts his hand on my shoulder. "But if you don't leave," he continues, "it may be the end of you and her."

The choice wasn't easy. In fact, I believe it was one of the hardest decisions I've ever had to make. Still, I decided I would go back in a couple of months. I would live in both places, and the travel would be intense, but I knew it was a price to pay to have my cake and eat it too, which they say you really can't do. So, I wanted to see if that was true.

Who could have guessed I would spend twelve years testing that theory?

Twelve years.

Wait, twelve years? I suddenly realize the gap in my fractured memory.

What happened during those twelve years? How am I missing twelve years of my life? Can you just lose years, misplace them, and hope someone returns them to a lost and found for you to reclaim?

I need a clue. I need something to retrieve those years from the rubble. Why are they hidden?

I decided to let my good friend Céline Dion guide the way.

"There were nights when the wind was so cold." *Yes, that makes sense. We were living in New York. Glimpses of the passing seasons. I see snow. I see years of Christmases. I see gifts torn into. I'm putting together toys on Christmas morning.*

"There were days when the sun was so cruel." Yes, memories of summers in NY and my time in California come back. I am still with the band. I am still with Elena. But to give 100% to one part of your life, another part suffers. Something caused this. Yes, Elena is part of it, but she's not the only reason.

"Did I banish every memory that was ever made?" *No, I wouldn't do that. That doesn't remotely sound like me.*

"There were moments of gold and there were flashes of light." *That's when it hit me.*

FUCK.

Slight Chance was reuniting to join a few bands from the late '90s and early 2000s for a tour. The tour lasted six months, and because things were different now, I was able to refocus some of my attention on the band.

"I have an idea," I say to the guys before we go on stage. "I want to play one of these songs tonight for Elena. Would you be OK with that?" I hold up my journal.

Everyone was instantly on board—like it was a treat, I was even allowing them access to this part of my life again.

"Which song were you thinking of?" Dax asks. "However, if I may suggest, how about 'Goosebumps'?"

"Really?" My eyes widened.

"I always believe that to know where you're going, you need to know where you came from. Not to mention, we've rehearsed it before." He winked.

We performed an incredible show. I remember it vividly. I recall Elena coming out for the show, but she wasn't alone…

Who was she with?

"Now, before we head out for the night, we have a surprise. We're going to play for you a never-before-heard song," Dax announces to the crowd. "However…" he begins as he starts to back away from the mic and over toward where I'm standing. "You won't be hearing it from me. Give it up for my man, Luke Grant!"

In an instant, the crowd erupts in cheers and applause. I position the mic in the perfect spot and take a deep breath. And like magic, the words feel as they did the first time I wrote them. And even though I can't see her face among the sea of screaming fans, it doesn't matter. She has always been my number one fan. And I will always be hers.

When the guitar solo starts, I take the liberty of flying around the stage with Jordan, energizing the crowd even more. Dax takes his spot back at the mic and fills the space with whatever vocals he can.

In front of me, I see nothing but the roaring crowd. The stage is like an infinity pool, and for some reason, I keep inching my way closer to the edge. The guys are in their element, we all are.

My guitar strap is draped around me, but I can barely feel it in my hands. I'm feeling the music as if it's lifting me off the ground. The crowd's cheers lift me even higher. Damn, I missed this.

As I turn around, I hear Jordan yell from the corner of the stage. He starts pointing at something behind me, but I can't understand what he's saying. For a moment, it's like he's trying to show how much the crowd missed us.

But he keeps pointing repeatedly with growing frustration until Monty catches on, and I immediately get caught in the middle of a babbling, incoherent conversation.

I take a step back, and suddenly I lose my footing. I fall off the stage into the crowd below. My guitar smashes against the floor, as does my head. I can barely breathe as the audience begins swarming me like bees. It's dark. I can barely see a hint of light, no matter how hard I try to dig myself out of the crowd.

Words are jumbled.

I hear my name. I hear the screams of the concerned crowd.

I heart my name again.

"Honey, I'm here…"

"Luke, you will be OK…"

"Dad?"

Then, it all goes silent as I'm brought back to a familiar darkness.

"Hello, Darkness, my old friend."

That's when the past twelve years vanish along with it.

Chapter Thirty-Two
Present

"I fell? Wait, I remember." I look at Monty. "Shit. I forgot all about it."

"I know." He places his hand on my shoulder. "It comes in waves, but that's why I've been with you—to help you fill in the gaps whenever you need it."

"Jeez. Twice? I literally had something similar happen in high school," I say.

"Yes. Remember when your doctor said to avoid another head injury? Well, you didn't exactly do that," he smiles.

"Clearly," I respond. "But explain to me how I'm missing twelve years of my life."

"You're not exactly missing twelve." He looks at me. "You're actually missing about fifteen. Twelve years you were gone, more than half the time. We released a few albums, went on some short tours, but it was hard for you," he sighed as if he struggled with recounting my memories. "You never moved back to California. You built that house, did some renovations throughout the years, and just lived your life. The fall? Well, that was fifteen years later than when you last remembered — not twelve."

"I don't understand. What are you saying?" I feel like I'm starting to black out.

"That article on your desk. Did you ever look at the date?" He looks at me. "We are reuniting after the fall. Or, at least, trying to."

"Let me get this straight, I moved from Cali fifteen years ago, and I fell when exactly?" My head is now in my hands.

"A month ago," Monty cut in. "It's been one hell of a rough month." He takes a deep breath as if the air escaping his lungs has been held captive for years.

The memory, like a prisoner, runs with an unfamiliar sense of freedom that neither one of us can hold onto

"She never left you," he explains. "Your memory was shattered into tiny pieces, yet you kept piecing together the ones that didn't quite fit. Somehow, you were caught up with her still being Dax. None of us understood it—especially since Dax is married. He has a family of his own. Do you know that?"

"But I have been trying to get to her for years. I don't understand," I say. "So, you're saying I have been suffering under a memory that isn't true? But what about this journey? I've attempted it many times before." I look at him.

He shakes his head. "Dreams. You've dreamt of this. You have never actually gone anywhere. The only reason I know is because you would tell me about it and then, well, you'd forget…"

There is a sadness in his words. He's literally been holding me up emotionally, and I had no clue.

"What the fuck?" I sit back in my seat. Now, I understand why Monty didn't just toss me back into the water of truth. I would have most certainly drowned.

I close my eyes, straining to remember what happened—not after the fall but before. The chaos of memories conjures up a tornado of emotional debris, but this time, I am in the eye of the storm. Abated breaths escape through my clenched jaw. Several times, I forget to breathe, but then Robbie unexpectedly reaches for my hand, signaling that he is still there.

"You were in and out of consciousness at the beginning. The only thing we knew was that multiple head injuries weren't good. We also knew there would be complications; we just never knew how bad," Monty continued. "The second one was worse than the first. Your mom and Elena wanted you to leave the band."

"So, wait, what happened with Elena, then?" I ask. "Why isn't she living with me? And no offense, but why are you?"

Monty blows another breath through his lips as they flap upon release. "She asked that I stay with you."

"We're together?" I can hardly catch my breath. "Then why isn't she with me?"

"You're married. Best man," he pointed at his chest. "Who would have thought it. Not to mention, I'm—?"

"Married?" I whisper, cutting him off.

"For a while, you kept reverting to your teenage self and not thinking clearly. You were getting angry with everyone. It was hard," he explained.

"It was sort of like déjà vu for her. It stung more than I could articulate right now because there was a bigger loss this time around," he sighed, looking from me to Robbie. "She even tried showing you pictures and your journal, but when you opened it, you told her it wasn't for her."

"I would never have said that," I say.

"But *you* did. None of what anyone showed you or tried to tell you registered. You didn't believe anyone. That's when you started to get angry, as I said. After you spent a few weeks in the hospital, you were able to come home, but pieces were still missing. You eventually remembered Elena, but from a different time, which is why you kept thinking she was still with Dax."

"So, my memories were all a lie?" I lean back in my seat. "Everything was a lie?"

"It wasn't all a lie, dude. It was just a little distorted. Still, you were recalling things pretty clearly so far. If anything, that's an amazing sign," he consoles. "I am actually shocked."

Shocked? Well, I'm really pissed off. I'm heartbroken.

The funny thing about lies is that when you're not ready to reveal them, they usually end up exposing themselves. And that's exactly what happened here.

Like a buoy in the water, no matter how many times you try to push it below the surface, it always pops back up. It's not meant to stay underwater; it's meant to stay above the surface—just like my memories. Yet, I was constantly pushing them down because I didn't understand what was trying to come to the surface. All this time, I thought it was all pain, but in reality, it was the truth begging to be seen.

Yet, I convinced myself that maintaining this lie was the only possible truth—that it would lead me where I needed to go. But in reality, it buried me.

As I sit in my truck, I start to put everything together. It all comes back to me like that typical wave, crashing into the empty parts of my mind. Only this time, I let it sweep me away.

I have often wondered whether my memory was playing tricks on me. Monty did it best to hold my hand through this until I was ready to pull back the curtain. However, I felt content being in a dark room. But what good was that? Now, here I am sitting in the light. I always believed, *With the lights out it's less dangerous*.

I just wasn't brave enough to turn on the light.

"So, the house," I begin, "Is it…?"

"Your house. Well, it's all of yours," Monty answered.

"And that's where I come in," Robbie interjects.

Chapter Thirty-Three
Now

Over the years, as I have refined my craft, I have lived for the lines that flood my heart with emotion. As a lover of music, I find the power it holds to evoke feelings ranging from sadness to happiness, or something in between, truly remarkable. Transcending, even. And the pride I feel from creating a lyrical masterpiece is unmatched by anything else. Well, almost anything else.

Writing the perfect lyrics and pairing them with the ideal melody is truly the chef's kiss—or rockstar's. Sometimes, something as small as a tune, a key change, or even the range in which a line is sung can create a kind of magic that can be felt in parts of you that you never knew existed. These are the moments I have lived for.

To me, Elena was always my heart's song. She was my masterpiece. She was sensitive. She was strong. She was my revolution.

As the buoy pops out of the water, the memory surfaces, and something once considered painful beyond words now emerges with hope and love.

I exited the truck with a bouquet of pink peonies (her favorite) in one hand while gripping the journal tightly in the other. I was back as a surprise. The band came back from tour a day earlier, and it was my idea to finally put my journal to use for our next studio album.

What I forgot was that the house was packed with people. We were celebrating a successful tour. Monty was there. Dax was there. I was the only one outside.

I was home.

As I moved closer to her parents' house, where she had been staying, I looked through the bay window of the living room and noticed a small child playing with something on the floor. It was a toy truck. A cartoon was playing on the TV, which no one seemed to be watching, not even the child…

"But I saw them together," I say, recounting the one memory that still didn't make sense to me.

"We had just gotten off tour a day early, and everyone came over to Elena's parents' house to celebrate. You were just running a little late because you wanted to stop and get her flowers," Monty says.

"But I saw them together," I repeat.

"Yes, they were together but not *together*. You are not remembering what happened correctly."

"Oh, yeah? And you think you know better? I retort.

"Of course, I do. It was me, not Dax."

"Elena ruined the surprise. She ended up telling me before you got there. What you heard was me talking to her, not Dax," Monty continued.

"What surprise?" I ask Monty.

"She asked me to be the Godfather," he answers.

"The *what?*"

"The Godfather," he smiles, "to your son."

For half an hour, we sit in silence. I feel like I just got off a carnival ride and was trying to regain my footing. I felt dizzy. I couldn't see straight.

When Monty finally turns onto one familiar street after another, I know I am finally home.

"Welcome back, buddy," he says as he pulls into my parents' driveway.

"Wait, we should probably bring Robbie home first,' I say.

"I am home." He smiles.

"What does that mean?" I look at him.

"Sorry, I mean, *Dad.*"

His words do not make sense. At first, I couldn't comprehend what he just called me. And when I start to, I see a familiar door open, and suddenly it all comes together.

I look at Robbie. He folds his lips into his mouth, and I know he is having trouble with words now. He climbs out of the truck and reaches for my hand to help me out.

"I heard all your stories, and I feel like I've gotten to know you even better. But if I learned anything, it's that if a hand reaches out, you have to reach back," he tells me.

I take his hand in mine as he leads me next door to Elena's parents' house (or, for that matter, his grandparents' house). He guides me to the front door where Elena is waiting. She looks the same as she did in my memory. Time has definitely been kind to her.

Her hair is tied back into a loose ponytail, and she wears the same flower necklace. She smiles, her green eyes as vibrant as the first time I saw them. Without hesitation, she pulls me into a hug. "You're back," she breathes. "I promise, I didn't leave you."

Her touch feels both familiar and unfamiliar at the same time. As she takes my hand into hers, I experience a flash of light. Every fracture in my memories has been filled in. I remember it all— from the moment I fell in love with her, the times we lost and found each other; the moment we said, "I do." I remember us building the house. I remember having Robbie.

Robbie?

"I am so sorry," I say to both of them. "I am so sorry I forgot."

"It was an accident—and it wasn't the first time," she chuckles as if trying to make light of things. "This time, I think we had a harder time grounding you to the present." She looks over at me at Monty, who waves from the truck.

"I just hope this never happens again." I embrace her tighter.

"We all agreed you need a helmet on stage—like you used to wear when skateboarding." She smiles.

"And you," I turn to Robbie, "I can't forgive myself for forgetting you." I am filled with both fury and sadness. It was one thing to lose time with Elena, but quite another to lose it with my son. I immediately thought of my dad and how he was never there for me, and look how I turned out? I am the same damn person. Maybe, the apple never falls too far from the tree.

"You never missed a game," he says to me as if reading my thoughts. "You always showed up to school functions unless you were on tour. You taught me how to play baseball—so did Dax, but he seems better at it," he laughs. "But music was my calling. I guess the apple doesn't fall far from the tree," he says as if mirroring my thoughts in a healthier perspective.

"And guitar really isn't my thing. Monty got me hooked on drums." He winks in Monty's direction.

Like muscle memory, parenting comes back tenfold. "And what is this about you quitting school? You'd better enroll in something or find a job," I scold him. "And how the hell did you get to the train station?"

Robbie looks over at Monty, who shrugs.

"Monty's idea," Robbie begins, "He said you were determined to come home, so we thought maybe we could help jog your memory. Who would have thought it would work? Although it was a nightmare having to remove all of our things from the house and acting like I've never been there. But I have to say, I really miss my room."

"Your doctor thought it would be like exposure therapy for the mind. Dipping your toes back into your memories like before," Elena interjects. "We knew this wasn't a permanent thing like last time; we just didn't know how long it would be. It was definitely much longer than before. So, we thought we would slowly return things as time went on and your memory started to heal."

"Yeah, and I wanted to help you remember. I wanted to learn everything about you—even the parts you didn't want to share. I also wanted to know why the hell you both named me Robert." Robbie looks at both Elena and me.

"R.L. Stine," Elena speaks up. "It's what brought us together."

"Like we-would-name-our-firstborn-after-R.L. Stine-fan, right" I chuckle, remembering Elena's words. "I'm so glad this is over."

Elena leans her body against the doorframe. "Well, you may deal with some memory loss later in life, but let's just focus on the present right now. We both know how precious it really is."

The present? What a gift. The past? A treasure. The future? A blessing. It's funny because I used to think I was a man of many thoughts, and sometimes, I find myself spending my days lost in them. I am not special or profound, but I believe that I have done my best during some unfortunate times. I always said timing wasn't my strong suit, neither was time itself.

As I stand there on the porch, I feel like the younger version of myself. No matter what happens or what life throws our way, Elena always helps me find a way back to her. To us. To our family.

"You have done so much for me." I look deep into Elena's eyes. "Yet, you have never asked for anything in return."

"What did I tell you? I don't need you to do something for me in return. I have you. That's enough for me." She smiles. "Are you ready to come in?" she asks.

"Sure," I smile. "I have nothing better to do." I wink as she slips my ring back on my finger.

I twist it as I enter, seeing a small flower etched into the band. *This girl really knows my soul.*

Epilogue
Three Years Later

The '90s never really left us. Not really. For those of us who lived through that time, it was too significant in shaping who we are to be forgotten: the music, the fashion, the culture, the lack of social connectivity—it all made us feel closer together. It's a bond we will carry in our hearts forever:

"Did you grow up in the '90s?"

"Fuck, yeah, I did!"

My life, honestly, is a mixtape full of all the songs that have shaped me into the man I am today. Love is life's greatest anthem, and when you find it, play that shit on repeat. There is no such thing as a broken record when it comes to love.

The guys are all in my home studio, selecting the songs we plan to include on our newest album, "The Stoneflower Revolution." Dax even adds a few songs about how he felt during our early years. It's a whirlwind of emotions from all sides of the awkward triangle I clung to for years.

As for Robbie, he'll find his way, whether it's through music or something else. Either way, he and I are closer than ever. For any parent, even a month without their child feels like too long. Just the thought of having my life back sends a chill down my spine. Maybe even Goosebumps…

14
SAVE
THE
DATE
15
Coming
soon
Book Two of the 90s
Nostalgia Series releases
early 2026!!
21
22

About the Author

Danielle is a born and raised Upstate, NY girl, living there with her two daughters, and Project Manager husband. She lives for '90s nostalgia and is currently collecting all things Clueless.

She never turns down Cinnabon, a hot Americano, and will steal your French fries.

She will forever binge-watch: *New Girl*, *The Office*, and *Sex and the City*. She loves to laugh and can quote "Dumb and Dumber" and all the "Ace Ventura" movies by heart.

Published at the age of 17, she has been writing has always been her calling, and she couldn't imagine doing anything else.

Other Books by Danielle

THANK YOU FOR READING!
DID YOU LIKE THE BOOK? LEAVE A REVIEW!!

I love my readers!
Join the Sweehearts club
for all exclusive content,

subscribe @
www.danielledexterofficial.com

You can find me

Instagram
@authordanielledexter

Tiktok
@authordanielledexter

Threads
@authordanielledexter

LOVE, DANIELLE

www.ingramcontent.com/pod-product-compliance
Lightning Source LLC
Chambersburg PA
CBHW011321310726
48973CB00011B/3002